ORPHAN UNDER THE CHRISTMAS TREE

BY
MEREDITH WEBBER

MILLS & BOON®

For my sister-in-law Caroline, an inspirational refuge worker

First published in Great Britain 2011
by Mills & Boon, an imprint of Harlequin (UK) Limited.
Large Print edition 2012
Harlequin (UK) Limited, Eton House,
18-24 Paradise Road, Richmond, Surrey TW9 1SR

© Meredith Webber 2011

ISBN: 978 0 263 22453 5

Harlequin (UK) policy is to use papers that are
natural, renewable and recyclable products and made
from wood grown in sustainable forests. The logging
and manufacturing process conform to the legal
environmental regulations of the country of origin.

Printed and bound in Great Britain
by CPI Antony Rowe, Chippenham, Wiltshire

Meredith Webber says of herself, 'Once, I read an article which suggested that Mills and Boon was looking for new Medical™ Romance authors. I had one of those "I can do that" moments, and gave it a try. What began as a challenge has become an obsession— though I do temper the "butt on seat" career of writing with dirty but healthy outdoor pursuits, fossicking through the Australian Outback in search of gold or opals. Having had some success in all of these endeavours, I now consider I've found the perfect lifestyle.'

Recent titles by the same author:

MELTING THE ARGENTINE DOCTOR'S HEART
TAMING DR TEMPEST
SHEIKH, CHILDREN'S DOCTOR...HUSBAND

These books are also available in ebook format from www.millsandboon.co.uk

CHAPTER ONE

SHE was a psychologist.

She should be able to look at a problem, consider it from all angles, and then solve it.

So why was Crystal Cove's annual bunfight of the raising of the Christmas tree causing Lauren Cooper such grief?

Easy answer!

Nat Williams would be there. Nat Williams, Crystal Cove's very own surfing superstar, current world number one, had been invited to press the button that would engage the ropes and pulleys that would lift the already decorated tree into position in the middle of the park that ran along the esplanade above the Cove's sheltered northern beach.

In her head, Lauren could hear her friend, Jo Harris, saying, 'But you're over him,' and Lauren was.

Totally, and years ago, and relieved to be out from under his spell!

Not even heart-broken, not even then at seventeen, so why now, at twenty-nine, did she feel ill at the thought of meeting him again?

Lauren, Crystal Cove's only practising psychologist, manager of the local women's refuge and general all-round competent person, rested her elbows on her desk, put her head in her hands, and groaned.

'Migraine?'

Wrong time and wrong place to be groaning! She'd completely forgotten she was at her desk at the hospital. The problem was she shared her office space with other therapists, and so it was open to any hospital personnel who happened to be wandering around.

She lifted her head and looked at the person who happened to be wandering around right then.

Dr Tom Fletcher, tall, dark, lean, and so handsome just looking at him sometimes took Lauren's breath away.

'No, I'm fine,' she told him as he pulled a chair over from an adjacent desk and settled down across from her.

'Really fine,' she emphasised, in case he hadn't got the message the first time.

'No, you're not.'

The words jolted Lauren out of her welter of doubt and anxiety and she frowned at him across the table. Eighteen months ago when Tom had first taken up his position as head of the Crystal Cove hospital, he'd asked her out, and she'd been very, very tempted.

But there was something about Tom Fletcher, with his grey eyes, easy smile and over-abundance of charm that had warned her to steer clear. Going out with Tom Fletcher might have meant getting involved. Getting involved might have meant...

She'd steered clear, reminding herself her life was just perfect as it was! She had a good job, a satisfying challenge in running the local women's refuge, great friends, family close by—the life she wanted for herself.

The life she'd *chosen* for herself!

As for Tom, well, her refusal hadn't dented his confidence. Since his arrival in town she'd watched him flirt with every woman in Crystal Cove; watched him squire any number of them around town, although none of the women he'd dated then deserted seemed to bear grudges against him, sing-ing his praises as a companion, their pleasure in the affair, remaining friends with him even after the relationships had ended.

Tom Fletcher, she'd realised very early on, was one of those men all women loved, and apparently he loved being loved by them, but he was of the 'love them and leave them' tribe with no intention of ever settling down.

And to be honest, she wasn't sure about the affairs or even his prowess as a lover because none of the women ever talked.

Which in itself was odd...

'Earth to Lauren?'

She stared at him, unable to remember what he'd said, and unable to believe she'd drifted off into her own thoughts while the man, apparently, had something to say to her.

'Sorry,' she muttered. 'What was it you wanted?'

You, Tom would have liked to say, but he knew he could never say it. Oh, he'd asked her out once, but fortunately she'd said no, because as he'd grown to know Lauren Cooper he'd realised she was a woman who deserved the best of everything the world had to offer and, as far as men went, that wasn't him.

'Nothing,' he said instead. 'Except to know if you're okay. You're pale as milk, you're sitting in an empty room way after working hours, and groaning loudly.'

She looked into his eyes and managed a wry smile.

'Not loudly, surely?' she queried.

'Loudly!' he repeated. 'It brought me racing from my office.'

Her smile improved.

'You? Race? Ice-cool Tom? The one who keeps his head when all around are losing theirs, isn't that the saying?'

'Well, I hurried,' he amended then because it was always so—well, *nice*—to be sitting talking to Lauren about nothing in particular—something that rarely happened in both their busy lives—he added, 'And you *did* groan, so tell me.'

If only she could! With a supreme effort of will, Lauren refrained from groaning again.

Although...

She studied him for a moment, considering the

bizarre idea that had flitted into her head—checking it from all angles.

Tom was a friend, after all, and what were friends for but to help each other out?

Although might it not be tempting fate?

'I *am* a friend.' Tom echoed her thoughts. 'So, rather than doing both sides of the argument in your head, why don't you talk it out with me?'

'Because it would involve you!'

Was it because the answer had come upon her so suddenly that she'd blurted that out?

'Aah!' Tom was grinning at her, laughter dancing in his eyes, mischief gleaming there as well. 'You've killed someone and need help to dig the hole to bury the body!'

She *had* to smile!

'Not quite that bad,' she admitted, 'although there were times today when I could have strangled an obnoxious eight-year-old who thought hosing all the girls who walked past the refuge was a fun way to pass the afternoon.'

'Bobby Sims?' Tom asked, and she smiled again as she nodded in answer to his query. One of the things that made Tom Fletcher so darned appealing—apart from film-star looks—was his empathy. He could sit down with someone and be on his or her wavelength within minutes, or so Lauren had always found.

'But you didn't strangle the terror of the refuge, so what's the problem?'

Lauren shifted her attention away from Tom—too distracting—looking around the room, feeling so ridiculous she wondered if she could make up some story to explain her groan and he'd go away and she'd find an excuse to just not go to the tree raising.

Except she *had* to go!

As her eyes came back to rest on Tom's face, he lifted one eyebrow, a trick she'd tried and failed to master in her youth, and she knew he deserved an honest answer.

'You'll think I'm stupid,' she began, then was furious with herself for being feeble enough to utter such an inanity. 'No, I *am* stupid. And pathetic, and ridiculous, and I've got myself into a tizz over nothing so best you just slope off to wherever you're going and leave me groaning into my hands.'

Lauren didn't do stupid. That was the first thought that came into Tom's head as he listened to her castigate herself. Of all the women he'd ever known, she was the most sensible, practical and level-headed, guided by what had always seemed a boundless store of common sense and a determination that bordered on ruthless—at least, where keeping the women's refuge open was concerned. As far as he knew, in her private life she was just that, private—she lived alone and seemed to like it that way—but stupid? Never!

'I'm not going,' he announced. 'Not until you tell me what's got you frazzled like this. Is it Christmas? Does your family make a big deal of it, so you have relatives who bore you stupid descending on you for weeks at a time, and people arguing about who's doing the cake and the best stuffing for the turkey?'

That won a smile, but it was wan and he realised that, subconsciously perhaps, he'd been worried about Lauren for a while. She was still as beautiful as ever, having good bone structure so tiredness didn't ravage her features as it did some people. But she was pale, and the dark shadows beneath her eyes had deepened so they had a bruised look.

The smile had dried up while he was thinking about her looks, and she was frowning at him now.

Quite ferociously, in fact, so the words, when they came, seemed to have no meaning—certainly nothing to connect them to a ferocious frown.

'I want to ask you out,' she said, her eyes, a golden, greeny-brown and always startling against her golden blonde hair, fixed on his, no doubt so she could gauge his reaction.

Challenging him, in fact!

'Okay,' he managed, though battling to process both the invitation and the fierceness of it, which made the slight start of pleasurable surprise he felt quite ridiculous. 'When?'

'Tonight,' she said. 'In fact, right now—we should be leaving any minute.'

'But it's the great tree raising do tonight,' he reminded her. 'We're both going anyway. The entire hospital staff was invited.'

No reaction beyond another, barely suppressed groan, so he took a wild guess.

'Do you mean after the tree raising? Dinner somewhere perhaps?'

He was speaking lightly, but inside he was a mess of confusion, though why he couldn't say. Perhaps because Lauren looked so unhappy, while her lips, usually full and with a slight natural pout, were pressed together, suggesting the tension *she* was feeling had increased rather than decreased after she'd shot out the invitation.

'I suppose we could eat afterwards,' she mumbled, and Tom had to laugh.

'Now, there's a gracious invitation,' he said, but no glimmer of humour lightened Lauren's face. If anything, she was looking even more grim!

He stood up and walked around the desk, squatting beside her and looking directly into her face, putting his hand on her shoulder—the lightest of touches but showing her without words that he was there for her.

'Tell me,' he said softly, and to his astonishment tears welled in her eyes, overflowed, and slid silently down her cheeks.

She made no attempt to brush them away so he pulled out his handkerchief, checked it was reasonably clean, and dried them for her.

'I *am* being stupid,' she muttered angrily. ' I have to go because of the refuge—it's been the main fundraising focus for the Christmas raffle and I'll be getting the cheque and heaven knows—well, you know too—the refuge needs it, and if Cam and Jo hadn't just become engaged I'd have asked Cam, but it would start too much talk in the town, and then there's Mike but he seems quite interested in that new young probationary policewoman, and the school teachers have all gone home for the holidays, so—'

'So you're stuck with me,' Tom finished for her. 'That's okay, I get the picture. You need a man tonight. That's fine. Do you want anything special? A bit of panting? Lusting? Public displays of affection? Kisses, or just hand-holding?'

She knew Tom was only teasing, but hearing it put like that Lauren wanted nothing more than to shrink to mouse size and crawl into a hole and hide. How embarrassing! How could she have asked him?

And trust Tom to make a joke of it!

But wasn't that for the best? At least he wasn't getting any false ideas. So why did *that* thought make her feel weepy again?

She hauled in a deep, steadying breath, and watched as he straightened up.

'I just need you to be there, that's all,' she said, cross with herself for making such a mess of things.

'But obviously with you!' he said quietly, and she, who hadn't blushed since she was fourteen, felt heat flooding into her cheeks.

Mortified, she pressed her hands to them to cool them, or hide the vivid colour, and nodded.

'No worries!'

But that was Tom! Nothing ever worried him—or seemed to...

He put his arm around her shoulders and looked into her face.

'Now,' he said gently, 'I know you're beautiful enough without it, but all my ladies go for a little make-up when they have to cover the signs of tears. I wouldn't like to think the entire population of Crystal Cove sees you've been crying about having to go out with me. It would do my reputation no manner of harm, so into the washroom with you. We've ten minutes or so before we have to leave.'

He turned her and gave her a little push towards the washrooms, catching up with her to hand over her big tote, which she'd left beside her chair, passing it to her with such a warm smile her stomach turned over.

Was she stupid to be doing this? Stupider than she usually was over men?

Was he stupid to be doing this?

Tom took himself off to the men's washrooms and splashed cold water over his face.

He'd been attracted to Lauren from the first time he'd seen her. Then working with her on the board of the refuge, he'd got to know her as a person and become, *he* thought, a good friend. So her refusal to go out with him had worked out for the best, he'd decided, because Lauren Cooper was a woman who deserved the whole deal as far as love was concerned and he didn't do love.

Oh, he understood it existed. It even worked for a lot of people, but to him it was the most destructive force on earth and he'd decided at an early age that he would avoid it at all cost. The women with whom he'd enjoyed affairs over the years had always understood there'd be no 'happy ever after' scenario ahead of them. He was always honest, explaining right at the beginning that he enjoyed women and their company, enjoyed the physical pleasure of affairs, and hoped the enjoyment was mutual, but that he wasn't looking for anything long term, particularly not marriage.

A few had asked why, and a few more had thought they'd change his mind, but on the whole they'd parted amicably enough and he remained on friendly terms with many of the women.

Lauren, however, was different...

'Are you having second thoughts in there?'

An edge in her voice told him she'd recovered a little of her composure, but he wouldn't have been human if he wasn't wondering what had rattled her so much.

He emerged from the washroom, wanting to ask, but the Lauren who was waiting there was so far from the tense and tearful woman he'd left that any words he might have had dried to ashes on his tongue.

Which, he hoped, wasn't hanging out.

She'd swept her shoulder-length blonde hair into a pleat at the back of her head, making her neck look longer, elegant. Mascara darkened her eyelashes, emphasising her fascinating eyes with their dashes of brown, green and gold, but it was her mouth that drew—and held—his attention.

He tried to remember if he'd ever seen Lauren wearing lipstick and decided, if he had, it must have been a pale, neutral shade, because one thing was for sure, he'd never seen those full, lush, pouting lips covered in a glossy, vibrant, fire-engine red.

A red that yelled danger, and beware, but at the same time tempted and seduced!

'Much better,' he managed to mutter, because wasn't he Mr Cool where all women were concerned?

Inside he wasn't cool at all, not even close.

Inside he was wired—his mind playing tricks on him, showing him flashing images of those lips while his body ached to feel them on his skin—just once—no, more than once—just once would never be enough…

'So, shall we go,' she said, *Ms* Cool definitely, whatever angst she'd been suffering, possibly was still suffering, hidden behind her war paint.

And it *was* war paint!

Those red lips would challenge every man who saw her, distract them from the tree raising, make them think things most of them shouldn't think about a woman they maybe didn't know.

She'd linked her arm through his elbow while his mind was rioting, and now walked him back along the corridor, and out of the hospital, her tote slung across her other shoulder, so her body was pressed to his, all down one side.

At least walking beside her he couldn't see her lips, although he did keep sneaking glances at them—at her...

Tom was obviously regretting saying yes, Lauren decided as they left the hospital building. His usual rattle of cheery conversation had dried up, perhaps because he was trying to think of some way to extricate himself from this situation.

And was the lipstick too bright?

From the day she'd heard Nat Williams was coming back to town she'd searched the internet for red lipsticks, wanting bright and vibrant red, not orangy red or pinkish red, but fire-engine red.

Challenge red!

And it had to last, not disappear the moment she sipped a drink or ate a sandwich...

She knew it was pathetic, still to be hung up over something that had happened to her teenage self, although the psychologist in her accepted that the damage Nat had done to her would probably never go away.

Well, some of it wouldn't—that was for sure...

'You usually chat,' she said to Tom as they crossed the car park, heading for the esplanade.

She'd spoken mainly to divert her thoughts, but also because it was weird, walking in total silence with the usually loquacious Tom.

He *was* regretting it!

'Struck dumb by your red lips,' he said, and something in his voice told her there might be an element of truth in what he'd said.

'*You* struck dumb by lipstick?' she teased, hoping they could reach some comfortably light-hearted plane before they joined the crush by the beach.

'Hardly!'

'You'd be surprised,' he muttered, then he seemed to collect himself, taking her hand in his and drawing her towards the area where the road had been blocked off, and seating erected to one side of where the big tree lay. 'Come on, we're in the good seats,' he said. 'I can see Jo and Cam among the crowd milling near the platform—we can sit with them.'

He pointed out the two doctors. Jo Harris was Lauren's best friend, Fraser Cameron Jo's new fiancé. But he didn't think Lauren was listening to anything he said, and was it because he was holding her hand that he felt her stiffen?

He turned towards her but her attention was on the stands, where a platform marked the place where the guest of honour would press the button to raise the tree. Tom checked out the people on the platform. Helene Youngman, the local mayor, four councillors, the managers of a few local businesses who donated funds towards the Christmas tree decorations, a youngish bloke in casual gear—was he the new dentist? Cam had heard someone had bought the practice but hadn't met the man.

Whoever he was, he had a woman and a couple of kids with him. And everyone seemed to know him so maybe he wasn't the new dentist...

Tom had been so engrossed in checking out the dignitaries on the platform, he hadn't realised that Lauren had dropped his hand. She had also stopped moving, standing there, a yard or so behind him, seemingly frozen on the spot.

She couldn't do it! Seeing Nat there with the woman who must be his wife had made Lauren's stomach turn over—not with remembered love but with remembered fear, *and* apprehension for the woman she didn't know. And most of all regret!

She should have spoken out—told someone—
anyone...

Got him the help he must have needed, although
at seventeen she'd had no idea help existed for men
like Nat...

No idea that there *were* other men like Nat...

Back then she'd blamed herself...

Tom had turned back, taking her hand again,
easing her towards the steps, and Jo materialised
beside her, grabbing her other hand, the fingers of
Jo's left hand squeezing hers, Jo's soft voice telling
her she could do this, giving her a quick shoulder-
to-shoulder hug, although Lauren was usually the
hugger.

They climbed the steps to the platform and before
Lauren could catch a strengthening breath, Nat
was there in front of her.

'Lauren Cooper,' he cried as he stepped closer,
arms out held for a welcoming hug. 'Well, probably
not Lauren Cooper any more. Far too beautiful not
to have been snapped up by some lucky man!'

Her brain misfired, synapses missing, catching in the wrong places, so she answered far too
brightly.

'Hardly snapped up—far too busy playing the

field! Wasn't it you who used to quote that tired old saying about why buy a book when you can join a library?'

She flashed a brilliant smile and pulled Tom forward.

'Tom's more a set of encyclopaedia than a single book. Nat Williams, meet Tom Cooper.' And for extra effect she pressed a kiss on Tom's cheek, branding it with a scarlet imprint, then reaching into his pocket, her mind reeling at her own outrageous behaviour, to find his handkerchief to wipe it off.

Fortunately for her peace of mind, because she was too shocked by how far she'd already gone to consider any further conversation, Jo's new fiancé, Cam, was a mad keen surfer and as soon as Jo introduced him to Nat, Cam commandeered the local surfing superstar, edging him away from the little group to talk waves and beaches and barrels and other surfing stuff.

Which left Lauren to face her best friend.

'What is going on?' Jo demanded. 'And don't tell me Tom knew you were going to introduce him like that. An encyclopaedia from the lending library! You made him sound like a hooker—or whatever the male equivalent of a hooker is. I was looking at him when you said it and he was as shocked as I was.'

'Nothing's going on,' Lauren muttered, not able to even glance in Tom's direction, fearful of the disgust she might see.

'No?' Jo persisted.

'Of course not! I panicked a bit, that's all,' she muttered angrily. 'Let's leave it, shall we?'

'Actually, I thought the encyclopaedia bit was great—heftier, more oomph, than an ordinary novel. And I don't know what they call the male equivalent of hookers—hooksters, do you think?'

Tom had materialised beside them, taking Lauren's hand in his and squeezing her fingers in the most comforting way as he joked about Jo's objections.

Still clasping Lauren's hand in his big, warm paw, he turned to Jo.

'Okay, Jo?'

Before Jo could reply—not that there was anything she could say now Tom had taken the wind from her sails—the mayor stepped up to the microphone and was urging everyone to take their seats. Tom tucked his hand beneath Lauren's elbow and steered her after Jo and Cam towards some spare seats in the fourth row of the temporary stands.

'I *am* sorry, Tom,' Lauren whispered to him. 'I don't know what came over me, and Jo was right, I made you sound cheap. The whole scenario was stupid—I can't believe I fell apart the way I did back at the hospital and put you in that position.'

'Hush,' he said. 'No talking. We're here to be an audience to the great and good of Crystal Cove, but do feel free to reach into my pocket for a handkerchief any time!'

For the second time in umpteen years, Lauren felt a blush creeping into her cheeks, but before she could apologise again, Tom was shushing her, whispering in her ear that they could talk about it later, not, he'd added, that there was anything to talk about.

Although they *would* talk, Tom added to himself. Lauren was his friend and for that reason he was very eager to find out just what the golden boy of Australian surfing had done to Lauren in the past to send the normally calm, cool and collected woman into such a panic. The Lauren he'd seen tonight was so unlike the woman he'd come to know during his time in the Cove that he could barely believe it was the same person.

The mayor finished her speech by introducing 'someone who needs no introduction to most Cove residents, world surfing champion, Nat Williams'.

The crowd gathered in the park and spilling out onto the beach let out a collective roar of approval. It wasn't often the sleepy seaside hamlet had something to celebrate.

Nat Williams acknowledged the applause very graciously, then brought another roar of approval when he said, 'It's great to be home and to see all my old mates again. There's no place in the world like the Cove.'

In fact, Tom decided as the big tree began to rise into position, it was obvious the people in the crowd were more excited about Nat's return than about the tree.

He peered down towards the front row of seats, picking out the blond head of the surfing great. Two small children sat beside him, and next to them a lovely brunette, long, dark locks flowing around her shoulders. She stood out from the crowd not only for her good looks but because of her clothes, a long-sleeved shirt and jeans when most of the women present, if they weren't still in swimming costumes with a sarong wrapped over them, were wearing strappy tops or dresses, minimal clothing as the day had been hot and the nor'easterly hadn't come in to bring relief.

He felt Lauren shift on the bench beside him and turned to see that she, too, was looking towards Nat Williams's wife.

And frowning.

Okay, so putting two and two together was easy enough—they'd had a past relationship, Nat and Lauren—but knowing Lauren as he did, he couldn't understand that she hadn't sorted herself out by now. She was one of the most sensible people he knew and her training as a psychologist must surely have helped her move on, but her reaction to the thought of seeing Nat again had been disturbing.

Could she still fancy herself in love with him that she was frowning at his wife?

Well, that might explain why she hadn't accepted *his* invitation to go out.

Although he doubted anyone as sensible and together as Lauren could still be clinging to some long-gone love.

Not knowing anything of love except that for its destructive powers, he couldn't really judge, but he had always pictured it like a fire—yep, a destructive force—but if a fire wasn't fed it died out—he knew that side of love as well.

So surely Lauren's feelings for Nat, unnurtured for however many years, should have died out.

His ponderings stopped at that point as an ominous creaking from somewhere beneath the temporary stand warned him of imminent danger. The creak was followed by a screech as if metal components were being wrenched apart.

'Get everyone off the stands,' he yelled, as he felt the faintest of movements beneath his feet.

'And everyone away from underneath or near them.' Fraser Cameron shouted his own caution. Cam was already guiding Jo towards the side aisle, telling people who were close to the edge on the lower seats to slide under the railing and jump. It wasn't far, less than two metres, but Cam was obviously thinking of lightening the weight on the straining scaffolding underneath.

Tom urged Lauren to follow Jo, telling her to

make sure everyone was clear on that side, then he began ushering the people sitting in front of him off the stands. The important people on the platform, which must have been more stable, were turning around, disbelieving and bewildered by the panic building behind them.

As the noise beneath became more tortured, metal bracing twisting and wrenching from its brackets, the noise above increased, so the aisles were jammed and people were jumping from the top level, way too high, while those on the platform remained in their seats, stunned into immobility by their disbelief that the stands could possibly be collapsing.

Tom thrust through the throng, ignoring yells of protest at his actions, and grabbed Helene, pushing her towards the edge of the platform.

'Jump,' he ordered. 'You've all got to jump. If the stands collapse all those behind you will come down on top of you, burying you and suffocating you.'

He grabbed the two Williams children, one under each arm, and hurtled to the edge of the stage, passing them down into the arms of a couple of helpers who'd appeared from the crowd below.

'Take them as far away as you can and keep people back,' he said, while behind him he could hear Cam telling people to keep calm, they'd all get off in time.

Which might have happened if the temporary seating hadn't suddenly swayed sideways, igniting fresh terror in the crowd. They surged forward, leaping over seats, knocking others down, adrenalin kicking in, urging flight from danger.

Tom kept hustling those on the platform to the edge, telling them to jump then run, but fear could sometimes freeze the body so some people just stood, as if unable to hear the urgent message he was giving, so he had to lift and carry them to the edge where others helped them down.

A sudden howl of protest from the scaffolding and the stand collapsed, metal tubing smashing through the wooden seats and steps, the stands twisting, spilling people everywhere, trapping some while pitching others into the air.

Tom grabbed Nat Williams's wife and leapt, hoping Nat was helping other people, though he suspected the surfing hero had been one of the first to jump, his wife forgotten.

'Thank you. I must find my children.'

She had a soft American accent and dark shadows beneath her eyes.

Maybe being with Nat wasn't all that much fun…

CHAPTER TWO

MIKE SINCLAIR, the head of the local police station, materialised in front of Lauren, as she and Jo were urging people away from the collapsed stands.

'We need to move uninjured people away,' he said, 'and set up an area for those injured.' He indicated an area of the esplanade, already closed to traffic. 'Jo, if we make this space a triage area, can you stay here and treat minor injuries? The ambulances will come through to here, while Lauren, if you can stay with those who were on the stands but aren't injured and those who have friends somewhere in that mess. Keep them calm. The Emergency Services people will be here soon—they'll have bottled water and basic first-aid equipment.'

Lauren understood her role and moved through the crowd, urging the panicking locals back from the stands, helping injured people across to Jo, telling the others to stay clear, comforting tearful women and shocked men, telling children they'd be safe, just to wait over by the tree and their parents would find them soon.

She was doing okay until she found Bobby Sims, rubbing furiously at tears he obviously felt embarrassed about shedding.

Bobby Sims, easily the most disruptive of all the children who were given temporary shelter at the women's refuge, crying?

'I've lost Mum,' he told Lauren, at first shaking off her comforting arm but eventually accepting it, *and* accepting a hug when she knelt in front of him and folded him in her arms.

He pressed close against her for a moment, then he lifted his head to say, 'She was right there.'

He pointed to where the jumble of metal scaffolding lay heaped with wood and people.

'Right near it. Greg was under there and he called out to her and she went and then it all fell down.'

Would Joan Sims have responded to a call from the man she was in the refuge to escape?

Lauren didn't know. She'd been running the women's refuge for the three years since it opened, and still couldn't tell which women would go back to the partners who abused them, and which wouldn't.

In the meantime, there was Bobby…

'We'll find your mum,' Lauren assured him, 'but while we're looking, will you help me?'

Bobby's startled 'Me?' suggested no one had ever asked him for help before.

'Yes, you. You know most of the kids around here from school. A lot of them will be like you— they'll have become separated from their parents. Go through the crowd and bring any kids who are lost or crying over near the tree. Once you get them there, they can look at the lights and decorations until their parents turn up to find them.'

Bobby seemed to consider objecting to this plan, then he straightened his shoulders and took off, hopefully to do something useful, not set fire to the Christmas tree or try some other devilment.

Lauren continued to herd people away from the stands, but the cries of pain and distress had her turning back towards the scene, checking, seeing Tom there in the thick of it, clambering over twisted metal to tend the injured.

Could the stand collapse further? Tom wondered about it as he lifted people trapped by the metal struts or wooden planks of seating. And had anyone been caught underneath?

Kids often played under scaffolding…

He sent a plea to the fates that this hadn't been the case and knelt to reach a man caught between two metal seats, apparently trapped.

'Can you hear me, mate?' he asked, leaning further in to press his fingers to the man's carotid.

The man didn't respond, but his pulse was strong, and movement of his chest told Tom the trapped man was breathing.

Tom used his hands to search for blood. If it wasn't pulsing out from any part of the man's body, then the best thing to do was to leave him so the paramedics could stabilise his spine before they shifted him.

'Can you give me a hand here?'

Tom glanced around to see Cam higher up in the wreckage, bent over another victim—male again.

'His legs are trapped,' Cam explained as Tom clambered cautiously across the tumbled seating.

Tom took one look and was about to tell Cam to leave it for the rescue crew when he saw the blood on the man's thigh. There was no doubt the man's femur was broken and his femoral artery damaged. They needed to get him out *now*.

While Cam supported the man, Tom began, cautiously, to shift debris from around him, trying to get at whatever was pinning the man's legs and trapping his feet.

A twisted prop lay one way, a wooden seat caught beneath it, and below both some scaffolding that hadn't moved, holding steadfast to its job, just when they needed it to bend a little.

Tom eased himself into a gap he'd found close by until his feet were on the solid scaffold, then he peered down to see if any unfortunate person had been caught below him and found the area was clear.

'I'm going to jump on this bit and see if I can shake the twisted part free,' he told Cam. 'Hold the bloke in case it all gives way.'

Cam didn't bother with a caution—they both knew if they didn't get the fellow out he could die before the jaws-of-life equipment arrived and the safety crew made the scaffolding secure enough for them to do their work. They were governed by all kinds of workplace safety regulations but Tom wasn't.

He grabbed the twisted bar and held it in his hands, then jumped, both feet rising then thumping back on the solid bar. Nothing happened, although he thought he might have felt a faint give in the bar in his hands.

He jumped again and felt the whole tottering edifice sway to one side then the other—sickeningly!

Maybe this wasn't such a good idea, but looking down he'd seen a lot of the scaffolding still holding in the section directly beneath him so he didn't think bending the piece beneath his feet would do much more damage than had already been done.

'One more go,' he said to Cam, moving so he could stand above the bar he needed to move and jump down onto it. Praying he wouldn't miss as coming down on it could do him a very painful injury.

Putting *that* wince-causing image out of his head, he jumped and felt the scaffold give, felt the bar in his hand tear away, so the seat was released and they could get at the man.

'What the hell do you think you're doing up there? Don't you know there are experts for that kind of thing? Have you got a hero complex, or perhaps a death wish?'

He turned to see Lauren standing far too close to the devastated stands, hands on hips, the fury in her words visible on her face.

'Lovely Lauren, don't tell me you're concerned for my welfare?'

Lauren didn't need to look around to know that plenty of locals had heard the exchange. She was sure Tom had known that too, and had said it as revenge for her demented 'date' ploy and the encyclopaedia reference. She'd kill him! She'd climb up there and do it now if not for the fact that another person up there might endanger him.

Him?

No, she meant the other people still up there. Cam and whoever he and Tom had been tending.

Didn't she?

She didn't have a clue, she just knew that seeing Tom up there jumping on the already damaged scaffolding had sent cold chills through her body and clamped a band of steel around her heart.

'The kids are all gone now.'

The voice, laden with doom although obviously the message was good, made her turn. Bobby

Sims was right behind her, fear and apprehension making his usually bright, mischievous face pale and tense.

'And I still can't find Mum.'

The way he said it melted Lauren's heart. For all his exasperating devilry, Bobby was still a little boy who loved his mother and had been with her through her string of abusive boyfriends.

'You stay with me, we'll find her,' she told him. 'If she's not around here, maybe we'll find her at the hospital. I have to go up there to talk to the people waiting to find out about their friends and family. We'll get something to eat and drink up there as well. The canteen will be open.'

To Lauren's surprise, she felt a small hand slip into hers, making her very aware that this wasn't Bobby, the torment of her life, but a little boy who couldn't find his mum.

She gave the little hand a squeeze, then knelt in front of him.

'I'll look after you, whatever happens, Bobby,' she promised, drawing him into her arms to give him a comforting hug, repeating the promise that she'd take care of him, rocking him slightly as she offered comfort beyond words.

To her surprise he not only accepted the hug but he hugged her back, although as soon as she felt he'd had enough, she stood up. She led him up the road towards the hospital, following straggling groups of people who were also missing someone they knew or loved, the night silent with shock so the whispering shush as the waves slid onto the sand sounded loud in the darkness.

Once at the hospital, she realised she needed to start sorting people again—telling anyone not in-jured to wait on the veranda so the nurses on duty and those who had come in when they'd heard of the emergency listed the others according to the severity of their injuries. Jo, Cam, Tom and the other hospital doctor were all at work, Jo and Cam in the ER, working their way through the patients. Tom, Jo explained as she splinted a sprained wrist, was in Theatre with a man with a broken femur.

After checking with the ER manager that Joan Sims hadn't been brought in, Lauren took Bobby through to the canteen.

'What would you like to eat?'

For the first time since she'd seen him by the devastated stands, Bobby's face lit up.

'I can have any of that stuff?' he asked, looking

at the offerings, hastily prepared, Lauren guessed, in the servery.

'Go for it,' Lauren told him. 'Grab a plate at one end and fill it up with whatever you want, but if you eat too much and throw up you have to clean up the mess.'

'Me? I'm only eight!'

'You,' Lauren confirmed. 'You're never too young to learn to do a bit of cleaning.'

She watched as he heaped his plate then put some of his choices back, settled him at a table, told him she'd be on the veranda and to come out there when he finished. She was about to depart when she saw shadows chase across his face and tears well in his eyes.

'No,' she said quickly, 'I should have something to eat as well. Wait here while I get some food and we'll eat together then we can both go onto the veranda.'

She grabbed a sandwich and a cup of coffee and returned to find Bobby had nearly finished his large dinner.

'There was apple pie there and some chocolate stuff and ice cream,' he reminded her.

'Go get some,' she said, 'but, remember, not too much.'

She was surprised to see him pick up his plate and carry it over to the servery, something she knew he refused to do at the refuge, telling whichever woman on duty in the kitchen it was a 'girls' job' in tones of such lofty disdain they knew he must be echoing at least one of the men who'd moved through his mother's life.

Back in the ER things seemed to be more chaotic than ever, but as Joan Sims hadn't turned up Lauren stopped in her office to phone the police station. She spoke to a civilian helper who'd come in to assist, telling him Bobby Sims was with her if anyone phoned to enquire.

The helper checked his lists.

'No one's called us so far,' he told Lauren, who was beginning to get a really bad feeling about Joan. She looked at Bobby, sitting dejectedly on a couch in the little anteroom where therapy patients waited, and had a brainwave. A lot of the OT and physio patients were kids so there was a TV, DVD player and a stack of DVDs in the small room.

'Can you work a DVD player?' she asked Bobby.

'Course I can,' he scoffed, then his eyes lit up. 'Can I watch one of those DVDs?'

He'd obviously seen the shelves of them.

'They're all yours,' Lauren told him. 'I'll be just outside on the veranda if you need me.'

She was about to walk away when the image of him standing there in front of the shelf made her turn back. She crossed the office and went into the little room where she gave him a big hug, then knelt so they were on eye level with each other.

'Are you okay to stick with me until we sort this out?' she asked him.

He nodded, then for the first time in the turbulent few years that she'd known Bobby he put his arms around her neck and pressed a quick kiss on her cheek.

'Have fun,' she whispered in his ear when she'd kissed him back. 'I'll be back as soon as I can.'

For some weird reason she found she had a lump in her throat and was swallowing it as she came out of the office into the corridor, slap bang into Tom.

'I was looking for you,' he said. 'Are you all right? Do you have to be here? Can't you go home and get some sleep? Someone should be resting—

there'll be a lot of fall-out over this and plenty of traumatised people for you to have to deal with over the next few days.'

He'd put an arm around her as he spoke and was holding her close enough for her to see the concern in his eyes.

For a moment she felt like Bobby—she wanted to return the light hug he was giving her, return it with interest because a hug was what she needed right now—but she'd already embarrassed Tom enough for one night with her encyclopaedia statement so she stepped away.

Practical Lauren returning!

'I'm fine. Have you eaten? Should I be rustling up some food for you and Cam and Jo?'

'We've people feeding us all the time,' Tom assured her, 'but it will be a long night. At last count there are about thirteen with serious enough injuries to be hospitalised, and another seven or so who need bones set, or stitches in wounds, then there are muscle tears, that kind of thing, strains and sprains.'

'No fatal injuries?' Lauren had to ask, although just thinking of it made her cold all over.

Tom closed in on her again, resting his hands on her shoulders.

'You're worried about someone in particular?' he asked, his voice so gentle Lauren had to swallow again.

Unable to speak, she nodded.

He nodded back, his face grave. 'There's talk of someone trapped underneath on the road side of the collapse,' he said. 'And from what I've heard it's unlikely the person would have survived.'

The pulsing siren of an ambulance stopped the conversation.

'They're playing my song,' Tom said, his voice lightening though his smile was grim, but he didn't hurry off, pausing instead to give Lauren a real hug—like the one she'd wanted to give him earlier. 'I'll catch up with you some time soon,' he said, and the words sounded like a promise…

The woman was so badly injured Tom wondered if there was any bone in her chest that wasn't broken, but he had no time for stupid speculation, he needed all his focus on trying to save her.

Crush injuries to the chest were common from appalling road accidents, and Tom knew the only way to deal with them was bit by bit. She had oxygen pumping into her, the pressure low so they didn't do more damage to her lungs, and her heart was still beating, which in itself was a problem, as it was also pumping blood out of her system through many torn veins and arteries.

'Sometimes it seems as if more's coming out than is going in. I've got the blood group done and we've sent out a call for whole blood but in the meantime the fluids should hold her.'

Tom looked up to see Cam gloved up on the other side of the operating table, ready to assist.

Two hours later they both stepped back, the woman, sadly still anonymous to them, beyond help.

'Should we have been helping with the other injuries instead of trying to save her?' Tom said to Cam as they stripped off their gloves and gowns and were washing together at the tub.

'Jo and your co-worker are handling them all—they were down to minor stuff when I left and I would think they've finished now,' Cam assured him.

They walked together through to the ER where Jo was slumped on a chair beside a couple of nurses, talking to Mike and another policeman. All of them turned towards Cam and Tom, took one look at their faces, and let out a collective sigh.

'We don't even know who she was,' Tom said. He turned to Mike. 'Do you?'

'Joan Sims—Jo and Lauren know her from the refuge. Apparently she's got a little boy.'

'Bobby Sims,' Tom said, remembering with sadness his and Lauren's conversation about the rebel earlier. 'I've met him before but he's always come in with a teacher or someone from the refuge so I hadn't met his mother. Where is Bobby now?'

'He's asleep in the little waiting room off Lauren's office,' Jo told him. 'Now all the other people who came in have been patched and matched and those not hospitalised have gone home, Lauren's in there with him.'

Tom turned and headed for the therapists' office, his mind on the small boy. He must *have* a father, although maybe Joan Sims had been escaping abuse by someone else.

Would the child be safe?

He felt a shudder, as if the floor had moved beneath his feet, and shadows of the past flew by like phantoms in the night.

Of course Bobby Sims would have family...

Lauren was sitting at her desk, her head in her hands, exactly as she had been earlier—however long ago this afternoon had been.

'Bobby?' Tom asked as he came into the room.

Lauren nodded towards the alcove and Tom walked quietly towards it and stood a minute, looking down at the sleeping child. He had sandy-coloured hair rough cut and tousled and a serious over-bite that would need braces before too long, but, like all sleeping children, he looked so innocent Tom had to brace himself against the pain.

'His mother died—we couldn't save her,' he said, returning to slump into the chair he'd left in front of Lauren's desk earlier.

'I was kind of expecting that. Mike came in earlier,' Lauren responded. 'He said she had horrific injuries.'

'Will you take Bobby back to the refuge until someone finds his family?' He wasn't sure why he'd asked, although it probably had a lot to do with the phantoms that had flashed by.

Lauren looked up at him, her eyes dark with concern.

'I couldn't do that to him, Tom,' she said softly.

'I couldn't put him in there with other kids who have their mothers. I promised him I'd look after him. I've all but finished my hospital and private work now until mid-January and when I have to be at the refuge, I can probably take him or get Jo to mind him, but the problem is my flat's so tiny and there's no yard and he's a little boy who needs lots of space. I could take him out to the family farm but my brother and his family and my parents are all away for a couple of weeks—spending Christmas with my sister in Melbourne. I was to go too, but—well, you know how low on funds we are at the refuge, and I've cut the staff and...'

Tom frowned down at her.

'That doesn't mean you should be working yourself to death there,' he muttered. 'But that's not the point, I can understand you taking Bobby home tonight, but surely you don't have to worry about a yard for him to play in—he'll have family somewhere.'

Lauren stared at the man across her desk. Eighteen months she'd known Tom, worked with him, attended various committee meetings with him, thought she knew him as a friend, yet there was a strange note in his voice now—one she couldn't quite put her finger on—not panic, certainly, but some kind of disturbing emotion.

However, whatever was going on in his head, she needed to answer him.

'Joan never named Bobby's father, perhaps she didn't know, and Greg, the most recent of the men she's lived with, is violent,' she reminded him. 'Like a lot of women in abusive relationships, Joan had cut herself off from her family, or they from her. Oh, Mike and his people will try to trace relations, but there's more.'

She took a deep, steadying breath.

'Bobby saw Greg in the stands right before the collapse. He was calling to Joan, and she went—'

'This man was underneath the stands? Did you tell Mike?'

Lauren nodded.

'He wasn't killed or injured there...'

She watched as Tom computed the information she'd just shared.

'Is Mike thinking—?'

'They won't know until the workplace health and safety people inspect the wreckage, but Mike's been to Greg's place—he's not there, or at any of the pubs. They're looking for him.'

A wave of tiredness so strong it was like a blow swept over her, and she shook her head.

'I can't think any more tonight. Best I get Bobby and myself home.'

'Stay at my place,' Tom offered. 'I've three bedrooms, plenty of yard for Bobby to play in, and I can dig out some toiletries and hospital night attire for you both as well. You don't want to be driving when you're as tired as you are, and if Bobby's still asleep you'll never get him up the steps to your flat.'

Lauren stared at the man across the desk from her, wondering just what the offer meant, then realising it was nothing more than the kindness of a friend.

She felt a tiny stab of regret that it wasn't something more, but shook the thought away. As if it could be that...

She even managed a smile as she made a far-too-weak protest.

'You don't have to do that for me,' she said. 'Especially after I was so rude about you earlier.'

He grinned at her and the stab deepened.

'I rather liked the encyclopaedia reference, not to mention putting the surf god in his place.'

'I doubt that,' Lauren told him, but the regret she'd felt earlier was turning to guilt...

'Come on,' Tom added. 'I'll show you where the hospital emergency packs are, or do you know?'

'I know,' Lauren told him, pleased to have something concrete to grasp hold of. 'I often bring in women who have left home with nothing.'

Tom nodded, so much understanding in his eyes she felt like crying, or maybe asking for another hug, but such weakness was definitely exhaustion so she hustled off to get some toiletries and night gear for herself and Bobby. She returned with her haul to find Tom had lifted the sleeping boy and was carrying him along the corridor towards the side door that was closest to his house.

Tom's house was the official hospital residence, built in the same style as the hospital with wide verandas on three sides, all of them providing glimpses of the ocean. As Lauren walked through the door she tried to think if she'd ever been inside the house before. She'd been *to* the house often enough, invited to drinks or a barbecue with other friends, but they'd always sat on the veranda.

The living room was comfortably furnished,

very neat and tidy, the only thing out of place a folded newspaper resting on the arm of a leather lounge chair. It was off to the left of the central passageway, doors on the right obviously opening into bedrooms.

Tom pushed the second door with his foot and it opened to show a pristinely neat bedroom, a single bed set in the middle, an old polished timber wardrobe on one side and French doors opening to the veranda on the other.

'Do you want to wake him to do his teeth and change his clothes or should we just let him sleep?'

Lauren considered the question—letting the little boy sleep was obviously the best solution, but he might wake and not know where he was.

'Not that I want to hurry you or anything but my arms might give way any minute,' Tom said, and though there was a smile in the words Lauren knew Bobby must have grown very heavy in his arms.

'I think we'll let him sleep,' she said, and she slipped past Tom and his burden and turned down the bed, then, when Tom put Bobby down on the clean sheet, she slid off his rubber flip-flops and pulled the top sheet over him.

Tom came forward and turned on a bedside light, using a button to dim it.

'All mod cons in this place,' he said, then he touched the little boy on the head and hesitated for a few seconds before following Lauren out of the room.

'Your bedroom is this way,' he said, pushing open the next door. 'There's a bathroom just beyond it, towels in a cabinet behind the door. Do you need anything else? Would you like a drink of some kind?'

Lauren shook her head, then common sense dictated she should ask.

'I don't suppose you'd have a blow-up mattress or a comfortable lounger? I'd like to sleep beside him in case he wakes up in the night and doesn't know where he is.'

Tom smiled at her.

'Great minds,' he said. 'I was intending to do just that, but if you're sure then it would be better for you to do it as he doesn't really know me except as someone who causes him pain when he lands in the ER after one of his wilder pranks. I do have a blow-up mattress from far-off camping days. I'll get it.'

He was about to walk away, but Lauren caught his arm so he turned back to her.

'Why?' she asked, adding, when she saw the puzzled expression on his face, 'Why were you thinking of staying with him?'

Tom's smile was gone, his face now pale and grim, although it would be. It was well after midnight and he must be exhausted.

'I was Bobby once,' he said softly, then he slipped his arm away from her fingers and disappeared back along the passage and into what must be the front bedroom.

His bedroom!

I was Bobby once?

What did he mean?

And why was it suddenly very important to Lauren that she find out? Find out all she could about the enigmatic man she'd thought she knew…

Why had he said that?

Lauren was a psychologist—she'd want an explanation for a statement like that.

But would she ask?

Lauren, his friend, would have, but this Lauren was different.

Because he'd seen vulnerability in her for the first time in the eighteen months he'd known her?

Because he felt, not exactly proud, but somehow pleased that she'd trusted him enough to show that vulnerability?

So he'd shared a bit of his?

Oh, please! Enough with the psychological delving.

He reached up on top of his wardrobe for his old backpack, assuming his blow-up mattress would still be shoved inside or strapped to it. He hoped the rubberised material hadn't rotted. If it had, Lauren was in for an uncomfortable night. Perhaps the reclining lounge chair would be more comfortable for her, although they would probably wake Bobby trying to manoeuvre it into the bedroom, and would it fit?

He tried very hard to concentrate on these nice trivial matters, but in his head the image of a little boy, younger than Bobby by a couple of years, tucked into a strange bed in a strange room—the first of a series of strange beds in strange rooms…

'Tom? Can I help?'

Lauren was in the doorway and it was obvious he'd dithered for so long she'd had time to have a shower for her hair clung in damp tendrils to her neck, and she was wearing what must be one of the ugliest nightdresses ever created. A vague purple colour, faded from much washing, it had something he assumed were bunches of flowers printed all over it, and it hung, shapeless as a deflated balloon, from her shoulders.

'Fetching, isn't it?' she said, smiling at the thoughts she'd obviously guessed he was having. 'Maybe the hospital insists on the design—it'd work better than an old-fashioned chastity belt for randy staffers.'

Though not for him, Tom discovered. Standing there in his bedroom door, freshly showered, totally exhausted but still so temptingly beautiful, his body would probably have reacted if she'd been wearing a suit of armour.

'You'd look good in a wheat sack,' he told her, hefting the whole backpack down from the top of the wardrobe and turning his attention to finding the mattress, shaking his head in frustration when it failed to materialise.

'Don't worry,' she said. 'I'm so tired I could sleep

on a barbed-wire fence. It's a warm night so if you wouldn't mind lending me that puffy-looking duvet you have on your bed I can fold it, probably in three—is that a king-size bed?—and it will be fine.'

Looking at the bed was a mistake. He immediately pictured Lauren in it. And it *was* a king-size bed but right now he didn't want to think about why he used a bed that size, let alone explain it.

'Okay,' he said, realising that the sooner he got Lauren tucked away in Bobby's bedroom the sooner he could sort through the craziness inside his head.

Could he put it all down to seeing Bobby in that neatly made single bed?

Of course he couldn't. It had started back with Lauren's groan, and the strange sensation of…satisfaction?…he'd felt when she'd asked him to stand by her.

Not to mention his determination to find out more about the vulnerability he'd glimpsed in the woman he'd thought was so together.

He'd stalled again, standing in the bedroom, only vaguely aware of Lauren walking past him and hefting the duvet from his bed. He reached out to take it from her, but as he touched her arm she dropped it, and stepped over it so she was close enough to hug.

For him to hug her, although it didn't happen that way. It was Lauren who moved closer, Lauren who put her arms around him, slipping her hands beneath his shoulders so she could reach around his body, then she hugged him tightly to her, her head pressed against his chest, a whispered 'Thank you for being there for me tonight' rising up into his ears.

Then, just as he was certain she'd feel his body's unacceptable reaction to the embrace, she pulled away, picked up the duvet from the floor, and left the room.

CHAPTER THREE

LAUREN shouldn't have hugged him, she knew. Of course she shouldn't, especially not without asking, but his words had sounded so bleak and there'd been such sadness lingering in his eyes as she'd stood at the bedroom door that she'd been unable to resist.

The problem was that now, lying on his folded duvet, smelling the man that had permeated it, she could still feel the tremors of—what, attraction?— that hugging him had startled into life. Tremors she hadn't felt in years but still recognised for what they were—definitely attraction!

In truth, she had always been attracted to Tom— what woman wouldn't be?—which was why she'd never accepted any of the invitations he'd offered when he'd first arrived in town. Attraction led down pathways she didn't want to follow. Attraction led to trouble…

And disappointment.

Even disgust from one man she'd gone out with—a man who'd called her names that shamed her even now to think about, a man who had been disgusted when she'd tried to explain it was terror that had stopped her, not a desire to tease and walk away, definitely not a wish to anger him in any way...

Go to sleep, she told herself, trying to shut down her mind, knowing she'd need to be ready for anything the following day. Above her on the bed, Bobby stirred, and Lauren reached up to touch his arm, talking quietly to him, telling him she was there and she'd look after him, although she knew he'd probably moved in his sleep and couldn't hear her words.

It was enough of a reminder of her responsibility to Bobby that it enabled her, at last, to stop thinking about tremors of attraction, and Tom, and the past, and drift into a deep sleep.

They were both still sleeping when Tom looked into the bedroom at eight the following morning. The revolting nightdress had ridden up so he could see Lauren's long, slim, tanned legs curled into the folds of his faded navy duvet.

Could he wake up to Lauren underneath that covering? he wondered. Wake up close to her, not practically falling off the edge of his big bed the way he always had when women shared it?

He shook his head at the way his mind was working. It was lack of sleep, and the uncertainty of the outcome of the collapse of the stands, not to mention Bobby's future, that was making him think things he shouldn't think. He should go across to the hospital to see the patients they'd admitted, but he knew someone would have phoned him if he'd been needed and, besides, he was reluctant to leave the house without letting Lauren know where he was.

Somehow the sleeping woman and boy had become his responsibilities, and he, who'd shied away deliberately from any responsibility outside his work, was finding it strange but no less binding for that.

They'd have to stay—

'Good morning? Have you been standing there all night? Scared one of us would wake up and pinch the silver while you slept?'

He looked down to see Lauren smiling up at him, golden hair tousled around her head, looking so unutterably beautiful and desirable his body did its unacceptable reaction thing again.

'Well?' the beautiful desirable woman on the floor prompted.

'I just poked my head around the door to see if anyone was awake. Would you like a cup of tea or coffee?'

He had to move, get away, stop looking at her, so he hoped she'd say yes to liquid refreshment, but instead she shook her head, said a brief, 'No thank you,' then sat up and checked Bobby as she spoke.

'But we do need to talk,' she added quietly, standing so the nightdress hem fell down to cover those long, slim legs most discreetly, and walking quietly towards him.

He led the way into the living room, knowing she'd want to stay within earshot of Bobby.

'So talk,' he said, and smiled when she stared at him, confusion in her beautiful eyes.

'Well,' she finally said, frowning at him now, 'I'm not sure where to start. Bobby first, of course, and probably we don't have to talk about him because Mike might have found some relatives but I'd be—I'd be unhappy about letting him go into care if there are no relatives—not right now anyway. And I know I'm not making much sense but Bobby's had a rough time of things lately, and somehow I'd like to think that even though he's lost his mother, once he's over that initial grief, his life might get better.'

The rush of words stopped abruptly and she looked directly at him, her gaze so deliberate Tom wasn't altogether surprised when she asked, 'What happened to you? Back when you were Bobby? Will you tell me? It's not idle curiosity, I hope you know that, but if you've been where he is now, then maybe your experience will help.'

Lauren guessed immediately that he wasn't going to tell her. It was as if he'd lowered shutters on his face, right there while she was watching him.

The memories must be bad—really bad for him to shut her out like that—and a tremendous sense of guilt that she'd pried swept through her.

Without further thought, she got up from her chair and went to sit on the arm of his, resting her hand on his shoulder.

'You don't *have* to tell me,' she assured him. 'I

should have known better than to ask. It was just that Bobby—well, you don't have to say anything and maybe I will have a cup of tea and if you don't mind staying here to listen for him, I can probably find my way around your kitchen and fix it for myself, would you like one?'

The words rattled out, her uneasiness added to by the tension she could feel beneath her fingers, Tom's muscles as tight as steel hawsers. But as she stood, desperate to escape the terrible atmosphere in the room—the atmosphere *she* had caused— he caught her hand and pulled her back and she landed in his lap, her face close enough to see the lines of tiredness in his face and read memories he didn't want to think about in his eyes.

'I'm sorry,' she whispered, touching that ravaged face.

'Don't be,' he said, then he put his head down on her shoulder, slipped his arms around her body, and just rested there, holding her, until she felt his body relax and his lips, surprisingly, move against the skin on her shoulder in what felt like a kiss.

He lifted his head—it couldn't have been a kiss—and looked her in the eye.

'Do you believe in fate?' he asked.

'I don't think so,' she said, 'well, not entirely. I don't think every single thing in our lives happens for a reason, if that's what you mean by fate.'

'Neither do I, but with Bobby coming into our lives right now, I have to wonder.'

Our lives? Lauren thought, but she didn't query it out loud. Tom had something he wanted to say and she didn't want to divert his train of thought, although 'our lives' had brought her tremors back again and, given that she was still sitting on his knee, the tremors were likely to get the wrong idea.

'My parents and my older sister were killed in a car accident when I was six. I survived and was taken in by Children's Services until a relative was found—a grandmother I'd never met because my parents had been cut off from their families. Cue violins for real Romeo and Juliet family feud scenario but they didn't die tragically young, my parents. They lived on to have two children *then* died.'

Lauren rested against him, wanting to hug him as she'd hugged Bobby, wanting to hug the six-year-old orphan Tom had been, but she held back, wary of distracting him from a story that sounded rusty, as if it was a long time since it had been told—if ever...

'It didn't work out with Grandmother, so Children's Services were called in again—and again, and again, and again. I wasn't the kind of kid foster-families liked—not quiet and biddable and appreciative of all they were doing for me. I was rebellious and loud and full of hate and denial. When I was fifteen I finally got lucky with some foster-parents who ignored all the horrible bits of me, and concentrated on some glimmer of good that no one else had found. Perhaps I hadn't had it earlier, I don't know. They were kind people—all of them were kind, in fact—but these two encouraged me to put all my anger and energy into my school work, hence the doctor you see before you.'

Long pause.

Should she break the silence?

But how?

Her mind had gone on strike back when he'd said 'Grandmother' and Lauren had envisaged a stern, upright woman who didn't know how to handle a bereft little boy...

A granny or a nana might have known—would have known for sure—but a grandmother?

Unable to think of a single thing to say, Lauren rested against this man she'd never known existed inside the Tom she did know, and hoped her closeness might ease some of the pain this delving into his past had caused.

He didn't seem to object. In fact, his arms tightened around her and they sat in warm, comfortable silence, and maybe would have sat like that all day had Bobby not let out a yell from the bedroom, which sent her scooting off Tom's knee and hurrying in that direction.

'Hi, Bobby,' she said as she walked into the bedroom, her heart aching as she looked at the sleep-rumpled little boy.

'Where am I? Where's Mum?' he demanded, the Bobby Sims she did know coming to the fore, belligerence written in his face, anger in the taut lines of his slight body.

Lauren crossed the room to sit on the end of the bed.

'We're at Dr Tom's house, near the hospital. You fell asleep watching DVDs and he carried you here.' She pointed to the rumpled duvet on the floor. 'See, I slept beside you.'

She inched closer up the bed, wanting to give

him a cuddle but aware he was holding himself aloof from her.

'The bathroom's just along the passageway if you want to use it, then we might all have breakfast.'

He bolted from the room but when he returned he took up his position on the far end of the bed again.

'Where's Mum?' he demanded, and Lauren knew she couldn't put it off.

She edged closer and took hold of his hand, and when he didn't pull it away, she shifted close enough to put her arm around his shoulders. Inside, she felt nauseous. All the psychology training in the world didn't help you tell an eight-year-old his mother was dead.

'Your mum was underneath the stands when they collapsed. The doctors did all they could to save her but she'd been too badly injured and she died.'

The punch surprised her, so his little fist slamming against her cheek sent her reeling backwards.

'She is *not* dead! You're telling lies,' Bobby yelled, pushing at her now, slapping, thumping-hysterical. 'She's not dead, she's not, she's *not*!'

Tom came in and grabbed the flailing child, holding him firmly, talking quietly.

'We're so sorry, Bobby, we really, really are. We know you loved your mum and she loved you, and although we can't replace her, Lauren and I want you to know that you're safe here with us and whatever happens, we'll always be your friends and look out for you.'

The words must have penetrated Bobby's wild surge of grief, for the child went limp in his arms and began to cry, quietly at first but then with huge, wrenching sobs that tore through Lauren's chest like heart pain.

'Give him to me now,' she said to Tom, who settled the boy on her lap so she could rock him in her arms, comforting him with soft words and soothing murmurs.

Eventually he fell asleep, and she tucked him back into bed.

'It's an escape mechanism, sleep,' she said as she joined Tom in the doorway. 'I wonder if I can take advantage of it and go over to my place to get some clothes. I can call by the refuge and get his things— Oh!'

She put her fingers up to her lips to stop any other ill-thought-out words escaping, and looked directly at her host.

'You might not want us here. I don't know why I was assuming we'd stay. Of course we can't stay— when he wakes I'll take him home. I might go over to the refuge and get his clothes, though.'

Now Tom put *his* fingers to her lips, startling them into silence.

'Do you know that when you're uncertain about something you rush into words? Is it to do with your training, or is it natural? A way of thinking things through by letting it all flow out?'

'I don't do that!' Lauren retorted, not sure if she'd been confused by Tom's words or by the touch of his fingers on her lips.

'Oh, yes, you do,' he said, smiling at her in such a kindly way she thought her knee joints might give out. 'And of course you'll stay here. I've just promised Bobby that we'll *both* look after him and you can't break a promise to a child. So scoot off home and get your gear, but I've already phoned the refuge and someone there will pack up all of Joan and Bobby's stuff and bring it here. Also some bike they know he likes to ride and a few books and toys.'

'You did all that before I woke up?' Lauren was getting the feeling that for all she'd thought them friends, maybe she didn't know this man at all, although as he'd once been in Bobby's position, maybe...

'I knew they'd be anxious for news of what had happened, and I didn't think it would be good for Bobby to go back there and see his mother's things. We can leave them packed away for a while—I've plenty of storage room here.'

Still bemused by Tom's forethought, Lauren hurried into the bedroom she'd been allocated, pulled on yesterday's clothes with some reservations, then came out, finding Tom in the kitchen.

'How long will you be?' he asked. 'Twenty minutes or do you want longer?'

'I'll be as quick as I can,' she said, 'certainly not more than twenty minutes. I don't want Bobby waking up and finding me gone.'

Tom nodded at her, then smiled and said, 'Breakfast in twenty minutes, then.'

They were friends, nothing more, Lauren told herself as she hurried across to the hospital to retrieve her car. And the Bobby-situation had put them together for a while, that was all. Besides, of all the men in the world she shouldn't get involved with, Tom headed the list. Tom was special, a great guy, an empathetic and clever doctor, a man who deserved the best of wives—something she doubted she could ever be.

Before the gloom from that thought could take hold, she laughed at herself. How had her mind flitted from staying over at Tom's while they got Bobby sorted to marriage?

They weren't involved, she and Tom, nothing whatsoever would be going on between them, except the well-being of a lonely little boy.

The house, which had become as much of a home as houses he'd lived in ever could, seemed somehow lonely after Lauren left. Having seen her off, Tom wandered back into the kitchen, telling himself this was a fancy and as he was never fanciful, it had to be tiredness and letdown after the drama of the previous night playing tricks on his mind.

The previous night! Could someone—this Greg fellow Bobby had mentioned?—have loosened the scaffolding some way? Could anyone hate another person so much they would risk killing many people just to get the one they hated?

He opened the refrigerator door, pleased he'd shopped the previous day, so he *did* have bacon and eggs, and in the freezer some potato cakes that fried up like the hash browns served at fast-food outlets. Bobby would probably enjoy them, although when Tom had bought them, he'd been indulging his own weakness for the fried-up slabs of grated potato.

But the idea of hatred had taken root in his head.

Did he not understand hatred because he'd never felt it—not even for his cold, disdainful, uncaring grandmother? Did one need to know how to love in order to learn how to hate? He'd accepted long ago he didn't understand love and was reasonably sure he'd never feel it. Not again! Not after losing his sister, his protector, the laughing, loving Jane. Much reading on the subject had confirmed his gut feeling that many children who grow up without being loved can't learn to love in their adult lives.

Not that he wanted love in his life—the screams of abuse his parents had been yelling at each other when the car had crashed thirty years ago still echoed in his head whenever the word was mentioned.

He shook off the strange mood of introspection and pulled the makings of breakfast from the fridge, but once they were set out on the table, the memories sent him back along the passage, to look in on the little boy asleep on the bed, tear stains on his cheeks.

'I'll fight for you,' he promised the sleeping child. 'I'll check out every damn relative the Children's Services people produce and if you don't like them, you'll stay with me. We'll cope, the two of us...'

But even as he whispered his promise to the sleeping boy, he wondered if he could do it. If Bobby stayed with him then he, Dr Tom Fletcher, would finally *have* to learn to love, because he couldn't let Bobby grow up as he'd grown up— fearing love, repelling any tentative advance of it, denying love, denigrating it...

He rested his head on the doorjamb and sighed.

'I can't smell bacon.'

He looked up to see Lauren at his front door. She had changed into a calf-length skirt, blue-green in colour, made of some light material that swirled around her legs. On top she wore a white tank top that showed off her tan, and framed there in his doorway she looked so lovely that for a moment he wished he *had* learned how to love.

'Come on through. I was just checking on Bobby. Have you got bags to carry in?'

'Bags?' she teased. 'I'm not coming to stay for ever. I've got enough in my tote to see me through a few days. Once Bobby's sorted...'

She'd reached him now and studied his face, frowning slightly. 'We *will* get Bobby sorted, won't we?'

She was seeking reassurance, which was so unlike the Lauren he thought he knew that he hurried to give her the same promise he'd given the sleeping child.

'Of course we will—properly sorted—no interim measures or temporary foster-homes or anything else. We've told him we'll take care of him and we will.'

He was pleased to see the tenseness in her shoulders ease, and felt a surge of excitement arc through him when she touched his arm and said quietly, 'You're a good man, Tom Fletcher.'

It was pleasure at her praise, nothing more, but he moved away, aware he'd have to be very careful to avoid opportunities for touches while Lauren was staying in his house. He'd always been attracted to her, and as he'd grown to know her over time, he'd been pleased she'd refused to go out with him, because he knew his attitude to affairs left some women hurt and the one thing he would hate to do was hurt Lauren.

Although with Lauren living in the house, perhaps…

He muttered several swear words under his breath, ashamed where his thoughts had led!

And as it turned out, he didn't have to go out of his way to avoid touches as they'd barely finished a late breakfast when people began arriving. One of the residential workers from the refuge was first, bringing Bobby's and Joan's belongings and some toys for Bobby.

'I'll put Joan's cases on the top of my wardrobe with other stuff,' Tom offered, while Lauren comforted the worker, who'd been friendly with Joan.

Mike came next, looking so worried Tom ushered him into a chair on the veranda so Bobby wouldn't hear the conversation should he wake.

'There's evidence the scaffolding was tampered with on one side. Some of the pieces of the shaped metal, clamps and elbows and such, that hold the bars together had been loosened enough for the joints to give way.' He paused and looked directly at Tom. 'We were lucky the outcome wasn't far worse. If you and Cam hadn't acted so swiftly in getting people off the stands, I hate to think how many might have been killed. But getting back to Joan, a couple of people have mentioned seeing Greg Carter under there, but we can't find him. We've put out an Australia-wide alert for his car, but it hasn't been spotted either.'

'What about relatives for Joan or Bobby? Have you got any further with that?'

Mike's shrug gave the answer. He turned to Lauren, who'd come out onto the veranda with a tray of cups and the coffee pot—refilled, apparently.

'Do you have any details of family members in the file at the refuge?' Mike asked her.

Lauren shook her head.

'Joan never mentioned anyone, but she wasn't from the Cove. The refuge did have her aunt as a contact person, but I remember minding Bobby for her some time last year while she went to Sydney for the aunt's funeral. We'd have a lot of Joan's details—Medicare number, driver's licence and maybe even her birth certificate. Do you want me to check what they have?' Lauren told him.

'No, I'll call over there,' Mike told her, 'but getting someone to put a trace on her details on a weekend might be difficult. Are you two happy to keep the boy here today?'

Tom saw the look in Mike's eyes as he asked the question, sending it into the air between the two of them. It was a look that suggested another question was hovering in Mike's mind—a question about whether the two of them were linked in some way.

Seeing each other and keeping it quiet—at least until now!

Small-town gossip was likely to link them anyway, if Lauren stayed on. Would it hurt her? Upset her?

Lauren didn't want to answer Mike's question. After all it was Tom's house, and he had promised earlier he'd make sure Bobby was okay, but as the silence lengthened she thought she'd better reply.

'We're happy to keep Bobby and we'll take good care of him,' she said, then felt her third blush in two days rising into her cheeks, because *she'd* linked herself and Tom together with that 'we', linked them as publicly as her staying on in Tom's house would in the minds of the townsfolk.

Red on the outside and cringing on the inside but it was too late to retrieve the words!

'Good,' Mike said, nodding, then adding, 'Well,

that's settled,' as if something more than Bobby's immediate future had been decided.

He'd no sooner departed than Jo arrived, announcing that she and Cam had called in at the hospital and she'd left Cam there talking to one of his patients who'd been admitted with severe lacerations to his legs.

'And what's this I hear about you two?' she demanded, turning to smile at Lauren before she added, 'Not content with borrowing the encyclopaedia, you've moved into the library?'

'We're minding a child, in case you hadn't heard that part,' Lauren told her, hoping she'd put enough ice into the words to prevent Jo taking her joke any further.

'Bobby Sims, of course, and he's definitely a two-man job—or a man and woman job.'

The grin that accompanied the words told Lauren her ice had done no good at all. Jo was revelling in the fact that she and Tom had been thrust together.

'Mind yourself,' Lauren warned her friend. 'One day you'll take that step too far.'

Jo chuckled, totally unabashed by Lauren's scold, and turned her attention to Tom.

'You look after this woman or you'll have me to answer to,' she told him.

Tom knew it was nothing more than light-hearted chatter so why did the words resonate within him?

Because he'd seen vulnerability in Lauren the previous evening, and it had disturbed him?

Vulnerability in a woman he'd always considered totally together?

Lauren, meanwhile, showing her more usual strength and determination and not waiting for Tom to reply, was telling her friend just where she could go and what she could do with her smart remarks.

'And since when did I need looking after?' she finished, but Jo just grinned a totally unrepentant grin and departed, heading for the hospital, although as she crossed the yard she turned back to Lauren.

'I'll do any shifts you were taking at the refuge while you've got Bobby. I'll phone you later.'

Jo was telling Lauren, not asking—evidence of their close friendship—but though Tom was pleased Jo would pick up any slack at the refuge for Lauren, it was the other phrase—to look after Lauren—that still lingered in his head.

It meant nothing, he told himself. In fact, having Lauren in the house was going to interfere with his life no end—he could hardly bring women here while she was here.

Not that his love life was important right now—definitely not with, well, not only Lauren but with Bobby in the house.

He'd promised Bobby.

Could a man have any kind of social life with a kid around?

Was he really so shallow that he was thinking this way?

And had he been wrong about Lauren all these years?

Did she need looking after?

He leant forward and rested his head in his hands and heard himself groan.

'Migraine?' Lauren teased.

He looked up and glowered at her.

'I don't know what's come over me. Here I am, a normal, easygoing male, doing my job, minding my own business, generally enjoying life and suddenly I'm making promises to a kid I barely know, and obviously losing my marbles altogether.'

'You're worried about Bobby,' Lauren told him.

'And worrying about him has not only brought back a lot of unwanted memories of your own but it's got you thinking far too far ahead. You're probably already worrying about how you can entertain your women friends when you've got a houseful of unwanted guests.'

He gaped at her. Was his head made of glass that she'd read through the knotted thoughts inside it so easily?

Then he glowered, because it was very uncomfortable having someone around who *could* do that, especially the bit about the women.

Although she'd missed the bit where he was worried about her as well.

She ignored the glower, held up the coffee pot and he nodded, and to top off the wild emotional swings he was experiencing, he found himself smiling because suddenly it was very pleasant to be sitting on his veranda with Lauren pouring coffee for him.

CHAPTER FOUR

TAKING care of Bobby consumed the rest of the day. He woke hungry and belligerent, and nothing changed throughout the programme Lauren and Tom devised to keep him busy.

They started with a surf, choosing the long southern beach so he wouldn't have to see the scene of the previous night's disaster, but the boogie board Tom lent him was too old, the surf too rough, the sand too sandy, and when, in desperation to find something to give him pleasure, Lauren suggested they go to a fast-food outlet for dinner, of course the one she suggested was the wrong one.

Back at Tom's house, an exhausted Lauren supervised a reluctant Bobby's bath, got him into pyjamas and was intending to send him to bed when she realised he'd slept until early afternoon and while she and Tom might be exhausted after a drama-packed night and long, exhausting day, Bobby was still running on a full tank.

'Can I watch some of the DVDs from over at the hospital?' he asked, and Lauren glanced at Tom who mimed a despairing 'Anything!' at her, so she took Bobby's hand and led him across to the hospital to choose a DVD he'd enjoy.

She'd been relatively surprised when he'd let her hold his hand, so it wasn't totally unexpected that he shook her off before they walked up onto the veranda where there might be people who would see them. But the fact that he'd let her hold it even for a short time heartened her, as he'd avoided physical approaches all afternoon.

'It isn't us he hates, just his situation,' Lauren said to Tom a little later. They were sitting on the veranda just outside the French doors from the living room, so Bobby could see them if he looked out.

'I wish he'd talk about it, even ask something,' Tom replied, speaking quietly, although the sound was so loud on the DVD Lauren doubted Bobby could hear them.

'He's blocking it from his mind. If he doesn't talk about it he doesn't have to think about it and he's very aware that thinking about it causes pain and grief.' Lauren sighed, then added, 'He'll work his way up to it. Well, I hope he will.'

She was expecting an objection when the DVD finished and she told Bobby it was bedtime, but he went willingly enough, cleaning his teeth first, then leading the way into 'his' room.

His little face was set, his lips tight, the tension in his body so obvious Lauren wondered how she might help him release some of it.

Giving him a hug and a goodnight kiss would probably result in another punch.

'You don't have to go to school this week if you don't want to,' she said, desperate for an opening that might encourage him to talk—*if,* of course, he wanted to. 'It's the last three days of term and nothing's happening so you can miss them.'

'Why wouldn't I go to school? It's the only time school's fun, this last week. We muck around, throw water bombs, so course I'll go.'

Oh, dear, the belligerence was still there—in force! Could she mention what had happened?

Gently?

'You do know the other kids will talk about the accident and it might upset you?'

His face tightened and for a moment she thought

he might cry. At least that would give her a chance to comfort him.

'It wasn't an accident.' The words burst from his lips. 'Greg *did* something. Have the police got him? Do they know he did it? Do they know he killed my mum?'

Tom had moved into the doorway of the room, no doubt intending to say goodnight to Bobby. Lauren glanced at him, aware the despair she was feeling would be written on her face.

To her relief Tom came closer, sitting down on the other side of Bobby's bed.

'The police know Greg was there and they are looking for him,' he said to Bobby. 'They'll find him.'

'Will they bang him up?' The little boy—and he appeared *very* little and *very* alone right now— looked from Tom to Lauren then back to Tom. ''Cos if they don't I won't go and live with him. He's *not* my dad, and if anyone makes me I'll run away and keep on running away.'

It wasn't that Tom was closer, he just moved faster, reaching out to take Bobby in his arms.

'We've promised you we'll look after you,' he reminded Bobby, 'and we will. We will *not* let you go anywhere you don't want to go, or anywhere you might be unhappy.'

The terrible tension was released. Bobby's tears this time were quiet and when they'd ended, Lauren and Tom shared the task of tucking him into bed, assuring him again and again he was safe with them. Then they kissed him, one on each cheek, Lauren telling him she'd be beside him if he woke up in the night.

'You want a story?' Tom asked, surprising Lauren, who'd brought in a book from the refuge but had forgotten about it in the emotional conversations.

'You'll read it?' Bobby asked, and Tom agreed he was up to the task.

Lauren left them to it, the little boy lying on his side, his hands clasped under his head, listening to Tom read a story about a boy who sucked his pet bird into the vacuum cleaner by accident.

Apparently it was weird enough for Bobby to enjoy it, although when she peeked in a little later, the child was asleep, Tom pulling the sheet up over him in case the night grew cool.

'Can we make promises like that to him—telling him we won't let him go anywhere he doesn't want to go?' Lauren asked Tom when he joined her in the living room where she was tidying up the mess Bobby had created while watching the DVD.

One crisp packet, one empty milk glass, one plate with one chocolate biscuit—melted and sticky— still on it, and various bits of torn-up paper he'd got from somewhere.

Tom watched in silence as she tried to piece the paper together, and when he didn't answer, she pushed a little further.

'Being Bobby, any relative they find could be the kindest, most loving and generous person in the world and he'd find fault with him or her.'

'I know.'

Okay, so Tom had finally replied, but 'I know' wasn't much help.

'And?' Lauren prompted.

Tom sighed and came into the room, slumping down in what Lauren thought of now as *his* chair. And that's what the torn paper was—the newspaper folded at the crossword that had been on the arm of that chair earlier in this tumultuous day.

'I think what he needs right now is reassurance,' Tom said, weighing each word as he tried to speak the random thoughts that fluttered like the bird in the vacuum cleaner through his head. 'If we can give him that now, while he comes to terms to some extent with his mother's death, then we'll deal with the next stage when it happens. Eventually, if a relative is found who is willing to take care of him, we will have to not only suss that person out but persuade Bobby to at least give him or her a go, but until Mike finds a relative, let's not worry.'

'That's easier said than done,' Lauren muttered, standing in the middle of the room with the tray of dirty dishes and debris in her hands.

Tom looked up at her and smiled.

'Isn't it always? We, doctors in particular, say don't worry to people knowing full well they're going to go on worrying. "Don't worry" must be the most ineffectual phrase in the English language. Now, do you want some real food? My stomach doesn't seem to think that a chicken burger and chips, most of which Bobby pinched from my packet, will get me through the night.'

'You can't go on feeding me,' Lauren protested. 'If I'm staying here a while, I should throw in for food.'

'We don't know how long you're staying,' Tom

pointed out, getting out of his chair and coming across to take the tray she was still holding in her hands—close, so close she realised there were dark rims around the grey of his irises, not to mention dark shadows of tiredness beneath his eyes.

'Let's get a pizza delivered, my shout, or Chinese or whatever,' she suggested. 'What would you like?'

Had she rushed into food conversation because a sudden sense of intimacy had crept over her as they'd stood—so close...

'Pizza for me, from the wood-fired oven place. You like pepperoni?' Had Tom felt the same intimacy that he'd backed up a pace before he'd answered?

'Love it, and plenty of olives and feta cheese and prosciutto as well, please, but I'm paying.'

'You're a guest,' he repeated. 'Guests don't pay.'

He moved away now, taking the tray through to the kitchen. Should she follow—wash and dry the plate and glass? This was the problem with staying in someone else's house—you never knew just what you should or shouldn't be doing. And standing with him in the kitchen—washing up or drying—they'd be close again. That probably wasn't such a good idea when an image of his eyes lingered in her head, and an uneasy reaction to his closeness rippled in her body.

She was still dithering when she heard him on the side veranda, phoning the pizza place, and then, from the snippets of conversation she could hear, calling the hospital as well. She knew he'd been over there for a while before they'd gone to the beach, and all but three of the patients admitted the previous night had been discharged. As far as she knew, none of the remaining accident victims were in a bad way, but checking again and again, she knew, was part of Tom's make-up. He was thorough in all he did, probably the most effective member of the co-ordinating team for the refuge, always coming up with suggestions and ideas.

The refuge! She hadn't given the problems there a thought—and what had happened to the cheque she'd been supposed to accept last night?

Better to think about the refuge than to think about Tom.

It was only the enforced cohabitation—what a word!—that was stirring up the attraction she'd always felt for the man, attraction she'd been able to hide behind what she considered a relaxed but true friendship, only too aware it couldn't be anything else.

'Pizza on the way. Would you like a cold drink?' She was still dithering outside the living room, lost in tangled strands of thought, so when he suggested they sit outside again and offered a selection of cold drinks, she allowed herself to be guided to a chair and said yes to a glass of the new low-alcohol wine a local vineyard was producing.

It would be interesting to try the wine but, more importantly, it was unlikely the low percentage of alcohol would weaken her determination that Tom should stay a friend and nothing more.

Unfortunately, it wasn't the low-alcohol wine that weakened her, it was the sense of well-being that crept over her as she sat on the shadowed veranda, looking out over the town towards the ocean, hearing the soft splash of the surf on the beach, seeing the lights on the Christmas tree, secured, fully upright, without fanfare some time during the day.

Not only well-being but belonging, which was stupid as Crystal Cove was where she *did* belong, having grown up in the hills behind the town. But this belonging was something different—an ease within herself, even though she wasn't alone.

And, no, it couldn't *possibly* have anything to do with Tom…

'What would make a man do what Greg Carter apparently did?'

So Tom wasn't thinking of well-being or ease—of course he wasn't.

Glad to have a new focus for her thoughts, Lauren considered the question.

'Perhaps Joan had told him she wasn't going back to him, no matter what he promised,' she said quietly. 'Joan's been a regular at the refuge since it opened and every time she's gone back to whoever was abusing her. Greg is the second man she's been with since I met her. It's a cyclical thing, abuse, but with Greg the intervals between incidents have been becoming shorter, which has pushed her to think more clearly about the future. She'd taken a part-time job at the local supermarket, and was determined to learn to stand on her own two feet.'

A sudden wave of grief for the woman washed through Lauren and she added, 'Sad, isn't it, that we've talked of Bobby and the future but not of Joan herself—not of a young woman killed when her life had barely begun and when a new and hopefully better future seemed to be beckoning.'

Tom shifted his chair a little closer, and reached out to take Lauren's hand, offering comfort as she mourned a woman she'd been supporting for years.

'I think that's something Bobby will be pleased to know later on—to know his mother was trying to make a new life for herself—although if it triggered the action that led to her death it probably isn't something we need to talk to him about right now.'

Tom heard Lauren sigh and wished he could do more, wished he could take her in his arms and promise her everything would be all right, but that was another of those empty promises—nothing more than words like 'don't worry', because who could guarantee 'forever' happiness? Life didn't work that way.

Fortunately the pizzas arrived before he could get too lost in the kind of introspection he usually avoided, finding his life was simpler and easier if he lived it on the surface and didn't delve too deep. That was how he'd survived as a child in care, never asking why him, or trying to work out how he felt about things, simply plunging into whatever life happened to have on offer at the time.

'Shallow, I suppose.'

He was pulling slices of pizzas, fighting with the cheese on top, onto his plate as he spoke.

'Do you prefer thick crust?' Lauren's question jerked him out of the rarely explored region of his mind.

'Prefer thick crust? Why would you think that?'

'You muttered something about it being shallow—I thought you meant thin.'

She was peering at him, a slight frown on her face, worry in her lovely eyes.

'No, you're hearing things, why on earth would I call a pizza shallow?'

At least the silly conversation made her smile.

'Okay, I'm hearing things,' she said, still smiling, and Tom decided that having Lauren on his veranda, smiling and eating pizza with strings of cheese hanging from it, was even better than having Lauren on his veranda pouring coffee for him.

Which, all things considered, was a very unsettling idea, given that even in his student days he'd hated having to share his living space with anyone. He'd worked all the hours he'd had available from lectures or study to pay rent on a tiny bed-sitter so he *didn't* have to share.

Another legacy of a childhood in care when he'd rarely had his own room, and had been made to share his few possessions?

He didn't know, and wasn't going to think about it, in case thinking about it confused him more than he already was confused. He'd just accept it, and it was only a temporary situation anyway, although…

'What if Mike can't find a relative who would be kind to Bobby?'

Lauren looked up so suddenly a string of cheese got stuck to her chin.

'I honestly don't know, Tom,' she said, frowning again, but maybe because she was having trouble unsticking the cheese. 'I realise your own experiences make you dubious about him being placed in foster-care, but we keep reading stories in the paper about really wonderful foster-parents, who've had dozens of kids through their doors, all of them turning out happy and well adjusted.'

Tom found himself sighing.

'I know,' he said, gloom descending to cloud out the happiness he'd felt earlier. 'Probably most of the foster-parents who cared for me were wonderful as well, but maybe I see myself in Bobby—the perennial misfit, resentful of kindness, suspicious of it, not understanding simple fun and laughter, always seeming to be on the outside, looking in.'

'Do you still feel that way?'

The question startled him.

'Me?'

Lauren smiled as she said, 'Yes, you. I think you do—I think you stay detached. We've been friends for, what, eighteen months? We've been on committees together, shared concerns over patients, been to parties at the homes of mutual acquaintances, yet I don't really know you at all.'

She paused, then added, a little sadly, 'Or you me, I suppose. Maybe we're both the kind of closed-off people who don't…well, not don't make friends because we both have friends and good friends, but maybe we're both people who don't share their lives easily.'

The conversation was, fortunately, interrupted at that stage, Mike pulling up on the drive beyond the front veranda steps, then striding towards them, the grim set of his face telling them it was bad news.

'The initial opinion of the experts looking at the scaffolding is that someone tampered with it, so

we're looking for Greg Carter as a murder suspect now. As far as Bobby is concerned, we've not
found any relatives as yet and with Christmas fast
approaching I doubt we will. Children's Services
have suggested he go to one of their emergency
foster-families'

'No!'

'No!'

Tom beat her denial but not by much.

'We'll keep him here. We'll manage,' Tom added,
and he sounded so positive Lauren knew they
would. Somehow they would cope with suddenly
having shared parenting—however temporary—of
a bewildered, orphaned child.

'My workload is down to practically nil, and now
Jo has Cam working at the clinic she'll help out
as well,' Lauren added, wanting to reassure Mike
that she'd be available for Bobby.

'And Christmas?' Mike asked. 'If we don't find
relations or a placement for him, what about over
Christmas?'

'I hate the word placement,' Tom muttered, and
Lauren understood it brought back too many bad
memories for him, but she'd already been planning
Bobby's Christmas so rushed in to explain.

'I was going to be in town for Christmas anyway, keeping an eye on things at the refuge then going out to my parents' farm after New Year. I'll keep Bobby with me then take him to the farm later in the holidays Tom'll be welcome there whenever he has time off—it's only three-quarters of an hour's drive so shouldn't be too difficult. If Bobby likes it there, I know the family will be happy for him to stay on when Tom and I have to work. I'll stay up there and commute, we both could, although if Tom has late nights—well, he always has the house and—'

She stopped abruptly, aware she'd been doing exactly what Tom had accused her of yesterday—rushing into words, saying things that had probably embarrassed Tom who undoubtedly had his own plans for Christmas. And now she thought of it, just where did Tom's latest lady-love fit into all of this? How come she hadn't given that poor woman a thought when she'd not only begged Tom to be her date for the tree raising, but had now shifted into his house?

She tried to think if she'd heard of Tom seeing anyone recently. Maybe a woman up the highway at Belrose? Or had that been last year?

Totally mortified now, she stared out towards the ocean, wondering why the human form couldn't vaporise itself and disappear…

Tom and Mike were talking so perhaps they hadn't heard her or if they had, had simply ignored her. And hopefully their conversation had been relevant enough for them not to have noticed her embarrassment.

Noises of departure brought her back to the here and now and she managed to say goodbye to Mike, but as he drove away she turned to Tom.

'I'm sorry, talking about arrangements without discussing them with you, including you in my plans when for sure you have your own plans for how you want to spend any time you get off, and another thing—I can't believe I didn't think of it earlier, but is my staying here going to get you into trouble with your girlfriend or girlfriends?'

Tom waited patiently until she reached the end of her apology—at least, she thought it was an apology although maybe that had got lost somewhere along the way—then he smiled.

In fact, now she considered it, he'd been smiling all along. She'd noticed his lips twitching while she'd stumbled over her words in her haste to get them out.

'Quite finished?' he asked, and she sighed, then shrugged and shook her head.

'I'm sorry,' she said, in case she hadn't said it earlier.

'No, and no, and no,' Tom said in a deep but gentle voice that coiled into her chest and seemed to clutch at her heart. 'No apologies are needed. How can you apologise when all you were doing was showing kindness and friendship? And, no, though I'm working over Christmas, I have no plans for my time off after it and would be delighted to spend it with you and Bobby and even go to the farm if your family don't mind, and finally, my sweet Lauren, there's no girlfriend in my life at present and even if there was, how could any worthwhile person be upset by you and I getting together to care for a lost and lonely little boy?'

Utterly relieved by his understanding, and perhaps a little excited by the 'no girlfriend' bit, although that was stupid, Lauren raised her head and looked at him, wanting one more assurance.

'That's all we're doing, isn't it?' she whispered.

Was it doubt that flickered in his eyes?

The same doubt she'd felt when he'd said it?

Was that all they were doing?

He leant forward and kissed her, a barest brush of lips on lips, yet her lips foolishly responded, clinging for a moment, wanting more.

Was she mad?

Fortunately, before she could decide, Tom straightened up and smiled.

'What else could it possibly be?' he teased, which wasn't reassuring at all, particularly as the coil around her heart tightened while her breath caught in her lungs and panic swept like jagged lightning through her mind.

She'd *wanted* the kiss to continue?

She sought refuge in her bedroom, where she dug her nightshirt out of her tote. What had possessed her to bring the one that had fat cherubs with bows and arrows—a gift from a grateful patient—all over it? She'd never really looked at the pattern before but peering at it now, yes, they were definitely Cupids. Not that nightwear Cupids could actually *do* anything...

Cupid was a myth.

But on consideration the Cupids were better than the hospital creation *and* the hot peppers on her other nightgown—the one her young nephew had given her for Christmas last year. Young nephew, Jake—Jake would be at the farm when she went up after Christmas. He was ten, a nice kid—nice enough to put up with Bobby's insecurities? She hoped so because that's all his bad behaviour was, an outlet for uncertainty...

And what was *her* outlet for the uncertainty besieging her right now?

Not thinking about it!

Ignoring it!

No other way to go...

She grabbed the Cupid nightshirt and her toilet bag and headed for the bathroom. Shower, clean teeth, bed, sleep— simple.

Simple, right up to the sleep part. She lay on the quite comfortable folded duvet on the floor and tried not to think about the man who owned the duvet. Tried to rationalise her thoughts—hadn't she known Tom for nearly two years, so why now start going gooey over him? Coils around her heart indeed! Although—

The although shocked her so much she sat upright on her makeshift bed and stared into the darkness.

No, of course she wasn't going to consider the although!

As if the fact that he wasn't seeing anyone at the moment meant he might want a brief affair with her!

But everyone in town would assume it's happening…

So?

So why not?

Heat coiled now, low and swift, reminding her that her body was meant for more than simply existing—it was meant for pleasure…

She sighed into the darkness—physical pleasure was something she'd read about often enough but never experienced, not with a lover.

A lover—that's all Tom would be.

An experienced lover capable of showing her physical pleasure.

A *very* experienced lover.

Could she do it?

She'd lost count of her blushes over this particular weekend but felt the heat rise again in her cheeks that she could be thinking such a thing.

As if Tom would be interested in *her*! Not after all the times she turned him down.

Not after he'd stopped asking...

And as if she could let it happen!

Lead him on then let him down as her stupid fears conquered her before they could even get close to physical pleasure?

No, she couldn't humiliate herself like that in front of Tom...

Tom lay in bed, missing his duvet, although it was hot enough not to need any covering. In actual fact, he suspected he was missing the woman who was sleeping on his duvet, although he could hardly be missing her in bed when she'd never shared his bed, and she was still in his house, so he couldn't really be missing her.

These musings having reached a dead end, he sent a silent apology to Emily up in Belrose whom he had been seeing in a casual, no-strings kind of way for the past few months. He mentally apologised for denying her existence earlier, though he knew full well Emily wouldn't be upset if their casual arrangement ended. In fact, he suspected she was ready to end it herself, or perhaps had ended it, refusing the last few times he'd invited her to come down or suggested he drive up for a visit.

It was a pity in a way about Emily because it was exactly the kind of affair he enjoyed—the woman far enough away to not expect him to be constantly dancing attendance on her, an out-of-town arrangement so no one was hurt by gossip, and a woman who had a healthy enjoyment of sex for its own sake, not wanting things he couldn't offer, like love or commitment.

He didn't have to consider love where Lauren was concerned, but he certainly had committed himself to her and Bobby for the foreseeable future. And apparently Lauren had committed herself to him and Bobby because she was including him in family post-Christmas plans.

She'd explain the situation to her parents, he was sure of that, so they'd have no expectations of him as a possible partner for their daughter—a future son-in-law.

Son-in-law? The thought of him being such a person was so totally out of whack he smiled into the darkness, then felt a little sad that it should be so foolish an idea…

But he drifted into sleep with the position on

his mind, wondering just what was involved in being a son-in-law—something he was never likely to be...

CHAPTER FIVE

THE next morning, as Lauren came into the kitchen, desperate for a cup of tea and a little peace and quiet before Bobby awoke, Tom looked up from where he was reading the paper at the table and said, 'Do you think we could give Bobby one really good day doing something special—just being a boy and enjoying things?'

Lauren considered it for a moment, then grinned at her host.

'Let's go for a picnic in the mountains. Up to Streatham. There's a Sunday morning market there with buskers and other entertainers—men and women on stilts, clowns, face-painting. We can go on from there to the national park and barbeque some sausages, have a swim in the pool below the waterfall, take a walk through the rain-forest—just have a complete nothing day.'

She looked to see how Tom was reacting, then remembered he had a job—responsibilities!

'Oh! Sorry! I should have asked. Are you even off duty?'

'You're doing it again,' he said, smiling at her in such a way the coils tightened once again—this time around her heart. 'Rushing into words. I've already been to work, beside which, I'm the boss, I can take a day off. Streatham's only a twenty-minute drive. If an emergency crops up, I can get back in no time at all. And if I'm not mistaken, we can get breakfast at the markets. Little *profferties* and German sausages and waffles and ice cream—'

'And cups of fruit salad and home-made yoghurt should we just happen to think the child needs a healthy breakfast,' Lauren put in, but Tom just grinned unrepentantly and reminded her that it was a day off so they should be able to eat what they liked.

When Bobby awoke he was wholeheartedly in agreement with the plan, even to the breakfast of the little Dutch pastries with icing sugar and honey and cream.

'And I can ride a camel,' he added, excitement sparkling in his blue eyes. 'Mum took me once and they had camel rides. Have you ever ridden a camel, Tom?'

Tom smiled at Bobby's excitement and admitted camel riding wasn't among his experiences, and then caught Lauren laughing at him when Bobby offered to let Tom ride with him.

''Cos you can ride with two people. Me and Mum did it!'

'It's good he's talking about his mother and things they did together, isn't it?' Tom asked Lauren, while Bobby was off getting his swimmers.

'Very good,' she replied, still smiling, presumably over the prospective camel ride.

But whatever it was over, that smile melted something inside Tom's body, softening his bones in some way—weakening his resolution to stand alone in life.

He had no idea why he should feel this way—no explanation for it, not even an understanding of exactly what had shifted—but he took it as a warning and knew he had to stand back a little, armour himself against thinking this temporary togetherness with Lauren—and Bobby—was anything other than a convenient arrangement for the sake of an orphaned child.

The Streatham Markets were alive with colour and music and people. Flags tossed in the wind, acrobats tumbled across a grassy area, avoiding the camels in their bright saddlecloths and fancy, plaited reins. Stilt-walkers towered above the crowds while stall-holders extolled the excellence of their produce.

'Can I have waffles *and profferties*?' Bobby asked, when the decision had been made to eat first and explore later.

'You can have waffles or *profferties* and yoghurt or fruit salad with whichever one you choose,' Lauren told him. 'You know all about good eating, and having fruit or veggies with your meals.'

'Yoghurt's not fruit,' the smart eight-year-old reminded her.

'There's fruit in this yoghurt and it's delicious. It's what I'm having.'

'Tom's having *profferties*.'

Lauren knew she'd lost but far more disturbing—after all, they could do good food later in the day—

was the strange feeling of not exactly family but togetherness she was beginning to feel. She, who'd always been so self-sufficient in her personal life, accepting that a husband and children weren't in her future, was finding this simple outing with a man and a boy extremely unsettling—emotionally so...

It could be tiredness or stress, of course.

Yes, she'd put it down to that!

But she didn't feel tired *or* stressed. In fact, she felt more alive than she had for a very long time—alive to the sounds and scents of the market, alive to the vibrancy in the air around her, alive, too, to the two males, one big one small, who walked with her through the narrow lanes between the stalls towards the *profferties* stall.

'Fancy coffee or plain?'

Tom's question broke into her musings. Just as well, for who knew where they might have led? She turned to look at him, intending to reply, and caught something in his expression—an unguarded moment perhaps—that seemed to reflect the pure pleasure she was feeling.

Weird!

'French vanilla if they have it,' she said, in reply

to his raised eyebrow, but when he smiled she knew she'd been right. He, too, had been enjoying their stroll through the markets even if he probably hadn't been considering the family vibe she'd felt.

They settled at a table beneath a canvas market umbrella, Bobby excitedly pointing out all the things he could see, telling Tom the camels were over that way.

'Sure you're not coming on a camel ride?'

For the second time on the outing, Tom's question brought Lauren out of a muddle of thoughts she knew she shouldn't be having. Mike would find Bobby's family. He'd be moving on.

'Sure of it,' she told Tom. 'I'll check out the fresh fruit and vegetables to stock up for the week. Anything you don't eat?'

He smiled at her and she found she had to concentrate on not panting, so tight had her chest become.

'Turnips,' he said.

'They're not in season anyway,' she told him, pleased she'd been able to answer calmly—pleased she'd been able to speak at all!

If Mike didn't come up with family for Bobby soon, Lauren was going to be in trouble. It had been okay fighting the silly attraction she'd always felt towards Tom when they met at work or with mutual friends, but living with him, being with him when he was relaxed and smiling and raising that darned eyebrow at her—well, how could her body *not* react?

She mused on it as she trailed through the fruit and vegetable stalls, then down the craft aisles picking up little odds and ends to put in a stocking for Bobby for Christmas—even if Mike found family, she could give him a stocking. But she was choosing articles almost at random because her mind was back at the idea of a possible affair. Dependent, of course, on Tom being interested, and then there was the thought that, although she was certain he was probably the best man in the world—he had experience on his side—to help her past her stupid fear of intimacy, might she be using him to get over this fear?

Loud yells brought people running through the stalls and though Lauren didn't want to add to the chaos, she had a sinking feeling in her stomach that whatever upheaval was in progress, there was a chance Bobby would be at the centre of it.

'It wasn't my fault. The stupid camel stood up too soon!'

Tom, seated high above Lauren on the camel Bobby had fallen off, confirmed that the animal *had* lurched into a standing position, back legs first, and it had been almost inevitable that Bobby should fall off. The unfortunate part was that he'd fallen onto the camel's handler who had let go of the reins as the pair tumbled to the ground, and the camel had gone loping off with Tom on board.

Someone had caught the camel, but with Bobby and the handler still untangling themselves and arguing over whose fault it was, no one knew how to make the creature kneel so Tom could clamber off.

Lauren couldn't help it. She began to laugh and soon all those who'd seen the fun were laughing with her, even Tom and the handler. Everyone but Bobby, who came and put his arms around Lauren's waist, whispering desperately, 'It really wasn't my fault!'

She hugged him hard—he was so good to hug.

'Of course it wasn't,' she assured him.

'Tom won't be angry?'

'Tom? No, he's laughing too.'

The second reassurance worked, for now Bobby smiled.

'It *was* funny seeing Tom bouncing up and down on the camel as it ran across the paddock,' the child admitted, making Lauren eye him just a little suspiciously. But even a little devil like Bobby couldn't have engineered the bolting camel.

Could he?

'Of course not, it was a pure accident,' Tom told her when he'd been rescued from the camel and Bobby was enjoying a ride on a small Ferris wheel.

'I thought so,' Lauren responded, then she turned to Tom. 'He's so insecure,' she said, 'so in need or reassurance, especially when things go wrong. It's as if everything that's ever gone wrong in his life, maybe in his family's life, has been his fault.'

Tom touched her shoulder, frowning slightly as he asked, 'Aren't all kids like that? I know I was.'

Lauren considered it.

'No,' she said eventually. 'As a child I never felt that way, and as far as my family went, no, I didn't ever think it was my fault things went wrong, unless, of course it was like the time I let the calves in with the cows and there was no milk the next morning.'

She thought for a moment, before adding, 'Later, maybe, teenage guilt stuff—I felt to blame for that,' then was sorry her thoughts had turned that way as it swept a cloud over the bright day they'd been having.

Though only for her because here was Bobby back from his ride and who could have clouds hovering over them when they had a child as full of life as Bobby was to entertain?

Laden with good, and a few not so good things to eat—every boy deserved a chocolate cake made in the shape of a spaceship—they left the markets, driving further up the foothills of the mountains, stopping at the national park and walking along the track to the bottom of the falls that splashed down in a thin silver stream from high above them.

As Lauren had been cramming towels and bathing suits for Bobby and herself into her tote she hadn't actually considered how she'd feel wearing her rather skimpy bikini in front of Tom. Yesterday at the beach, she'd worn her other bathers—a decorous blue swimsuit that she wore for exercise swims—but it had still been wet this morning hence the bikini.

What she also hadn't considered was the effect

seeing Tom in his swimming trunks would have on her body. Yesterday he'd been in the water with Bobby so she hadn't had a lot of time to take in broad shoulders that sloped to a narrow waist and hips, pecs a weightlifter would be proud of, a six-pack—yes, definitely defined—and a flat stomach she could only envy.

He had the most beautiful male body she had ever seen, and she was positively gawping at it.

Gawping at it and thinking things she shouldn't think about it—about how it would feel to touch the skin that slid tightly over those muscles—and how touching it would make *her* feel…

Fortunately Tom was busy explaining to Bobby that the he couldn't climb the rock beside the waterfall and jump in because you never knew what was under the water in creeks and waterholes and you could be badly injured, so she could afford a little gawp.

'Or dead?' Bobby asked Tom, reminding Lauren she had too many responsibilities right now to be considering chest appeal.

She studied the child, wondering if the question was prompted by thoughts of his mother, but as he didn't elaborate, she decided it must have been nothing more than a casual remark.

The boy and the man with the chest she wasn't going to look at any more slid carefully into the water, shrieking at the icy coldness of it, splashing and shouting so the rainforest all around came alive with the joyous noise.

And once again a strange feeling stole over Lauren—a feeling of family—of belonging—of wanting something she'd always told herself she didn't want—convincing herself she didn't want it because she knew she couldn't have it...

Icy water should have the same effect as cold showers, Tom told himself, as he shivered in the green depths of the mountain pool. One look at Lauren in the silky scarlet bikini that hinted at more than it covered and his body had forgotten she was just a friend, and also that, at the moment anyway, he was in a position where he couldn't do anything about any lust or attraction he might feel.

She was a guest in his house and therefore off limits.

'I can dive!'

Bobby's declaration brought his mind back onto his responsibilities. The kid hadn't climbed the high rock, but he was out of the pool, standing on the bank, arms raised for a dive.

'Let me check first,' Tom told him, and he swam beneath the cool green water, checking there were no hidden obstacles that could injure Bobby as he entered the water.

'Okay, it's all clear, but always check. Will you remember that?'

Bobby grinned at him.

'Always check! I'll remember!'

Then he belly-flopped into the water, sinking under the surface then emerging in a mass of bubbles, arms and legs, shrieking his delight so loudly Tom heard the beat of wings as birds in surrounding trees took flight.

But the sheer joy of the child tugged at something deep inside Tom's heart, and whatever the something was, it niggled around and disturbed all the comfortable decisions he'd made about what he wanted out of life. No hassles, no complications—he'd never added no children because he'd never considered marriage, but...

'Can you dive?' Bobby asked, his face shiny with water and his eyes gleaming with excitement.

'I can but I'm not going to dive into the pool even

though I've checked the bottom because it's a bit shallow for me. If I hit my head I could break my neck and be paralysed for life—that's the kind of terrible accident you can have from something as simple as diving into a pool.'

He was talking to air by the time he'd finished his instructive mini-lecture, Bobby now swimming underwater, bubbles rising to the surface to show his progress.

Still bubbles rising, but hadn't he been down there too long?

How long was too long?

How did parents know these things?

Bobby burst to the surface with a loud 'Did you see that?' and relief washed through Tom's body. He was assuring Bobby that he *had* seen it and had been very impressed when out of the corner of his eye he saw a blonde sylph in a scarlet bikini sliding into the water. Were sylphs water beings or did he mean sprites? Naiads? Nymphs? Whatever! The name no longer mattered as Lauren slipped into the water and swam towards him, starting all the unacceptable reactions again.

Sleek as a seal, she swam his way then, thank you, Lord, turned to grab Bobby's legs and tumble him over in the water. Tom eased back onto the bank of the creek and watched the pair play, Bobby's joy so palpable Tom felt a rush of pleasure that he'd had a part in providing it.

But there'd be other days when joy was absent, Tom reminded himself. Not all day perhaps, but at least for part of them. No one could promise unending joy. Was that where parents came in? Could they act as buffers in the bad times? He realised they couldn't protect their child or children from every hurt or worry but they could help them cope with things that happened to them?

He slid into the water again, reminding himself Bobby wasn't going to be his long-term responsibility so he didn't have to consider things like this. To his surprise, he found *that* thought profoundly depressing and it was only Bobby leaping onto his back and trying to duck him that brought him back to laughter.

Sensing the swim was nearly over—Bobby was getting cold—Lauren slipped from the water and pulled on her long shift, too embarrassed to have her body on view to Tom for longer than was absolutely necessary. She carried the picnic basket over to a table near a gas-fired barbecue, and began to unpack it.

'Did you bring drinks?' Bobby demanded, arriving, towel-wrapped, beside her.

'Juice or water, both in the cool box,' Lauren told him, and ignored his grumbles, knowing he was used to drinking fruit juice because it was all they had at the refuge, although fizzy soft drinks were allowed on treat nights.

Bobby chose water then he sidled up to Lauren. 'Can I help?'

She was so surprised she had to repeat the request in her head in order to process it. This was Bobby, the child who refused to help in any household chores.

'You can set the table for me,' she told him. 'There's a cloth in the picnic basket, and some plastic plates, and the sauce and bread.'

And to her further surprise Bobby set the table beautifully, spreading out the cloth, laying out the plates, shifting things here and there until satisfied with his arrangement.

'Where's Tom, did you drown him?' she asked, then immediately regretted the joke as Bobby's face quivered with alarm.

'Here's Tom!' The missing man emerged from the trees near the waterfall.

'I thought I saw something there and wanted to check. Have you ever seen a tawny frogmouth owl, Bobby?'

'An owl? A bird owl?' Bobby asked, so much disbelief in his voice Lauren had to smile.

'An owl,' Tom confirmed. 'Well, we call them owls although they are really a bird like a nightjar. Come and look while the barbecue is heating up! There are three of them, the parents and a youngster, in a tree near the waterfall. They must have a nest there. Tawny frogmouths use the same nest for their eggs every year.'

Tom led them along a track through trees, eventually stopping in a clearing and pointing up at the three birds sitting on the branch of a tree. The two adults had their beaks pointed upwards so they looked like two small branches, but the little fledgling was still practising this manoeuvre and kept moving.

'Are those two big ones really birds?' Bobby asked, and just then one of them moved, peering down at the onlookers before taking up his statue pose again.

They stood quietly, watching the birds, Bobby obviously intrigued, asking questions about nests and eggs and how Tom had spotted them.

'I was lying on my back in the pool and one of them must have moved and caught my eye so I had a closer look,' Tom explained.

'I'm glad you found them,' Bobby said. 'I've never seen birds before—well, I've seen birds but not owls or whatever they are, not sitting like that so near and all.'

He turned and grinned at his two adult companions.

'If they live there all the time, we could see them every time we come here, and maybe they'll get to know us and we could give them mice or something good for them to eat,' Bobby said.

Lauren knew she'd stiffened, and felt Tom's shock as well—a realisation that things were getting more complicated than they'd intended.

'I think they eat insects or maybe mice,' Tom said, and Lauren took his hand and squeezed it gratefully.

'Good recovery,' she whispered, as Bobby darted back towards the barbecue. 'But we probably need to think about how he's seeing this temporary care arrangement. We don't want him hurt again, losing us as carers…'

Her voice trailed off because she knew that wasn't exactly what she'd meant. What had shocked her was how much *she'd* felt the family vibe, as the three of them had delighted in something as simple as a family of birds sitting in a tree.

The situation was rife with danger, and not just the danger of more damage to Bobby's security. Danger that became instantly apparent when, perhaps in response to the family vibe, Tom brushed his hand across her shoulder, somehow turning her, so once again, as if some unseen puppeteer was manoeuvring both their bodies, their lips met. The coil around Lauren's heart tightened, but it was the heat that flared within her that shocked her most, making her press herself against Tom to ease the pain of it. His arms held her close, and as their lips parted and the taste of Tom turned heat to scorching need, she lost herself in feeling, freezing only when his hand touched the outside of her shift above her breast—

'The sausages are cooked!'

Bobby's voice brought her back to her senses,

although she couldn't look at Tom, aware she'd backed away far too quickly, breaking from his arms with a forceful, panicked push.

Aware he must be wondering what on earth was going on...

But danger was forgotten as they ate sausages in bread with lashings of tomato sauce, and followed up with chocolate rocket cake. They walked off this repast by climbing to the top of the waterfall, up a slippery slope with spray cooling the climb.

'Home time,' Tom said eventually, and after visiting the owls once more, they drove back to town as the sun was setting behind the mountains.

Tom offered to supervise Bobby's bath '—I don't need one, I've been swimming!—' while Lauren unpacked the picnic basket and fixed toasted sandwiches for tea. The message light was flashing on Tom's phone but she ignored it, having phoned the refuge from her mobile earlier to assure herself all was well there.

It wasn't until Bobby was asleep in bed that Tom checked his messages. Lauren was cleaning up their supper things so heard Mike's voice on the answering-machine.

'Still no joy in finding any of Bobby's relations,'

he said. 'Are you two okay to keep him a little longer?'

More than happy as far as he was concerned, Tom answered silently, but the disturbing part of the message was the way Mike had linked them. 'Are you two okay to keep him?' Mike had said it as if they were a couple, and not only that but Tom had quite liked the way it had sounded.

Given the fact that all he'd wanted, all his life, had been to live alone, that reaction was disturbing. Oh, as he'd grown older he'd realised the value of friendship and had some good, even close friends, and naturally as he'd matured he'd learnt the pleasures of female company and again had made arrangements that fitted in with the life he'd planned all those years ago.

And he'd been happy—he knew he had been—so why were silly incidents like looking at a family of tawny frogmouth birds, not to mention a casual kiss, disturbing him?

'*Are* we okay keeping him?'

At least she had emphasised the 'are', not the 'we', although the 'we' disturbed him in the same way the moments near the tawny frogmouths had.

'Of course,' Tom told her, ignoring concerns

multiplying in his head. 'Well, I am, anyway, for as long as possible. He needs a bit of stability right now.'

Lauren smiled at him and whether it was the relaxing day, or the memory of what had happened *after* they'd been watching the owls, the smile started a different warmth from the one he was becoming used to feeling in Lauren's presence.

It was a pleasant, gentle warmth, spreading easily through his body, not zeroing like heat downward to his groin.

Not desire at all, just warmth…

Very strange!

'I think I'll turn in now,' Lauren said, hovering in the kitchen.

'No, it's far too early. Join me for a nightcap on the veranda. I've a lovely chocolate liqueur, or a very nice old malt whisky. Just a snifter?'

Another smile and a nod of agreement.

'But no drink,' she said. 'I'm just as happy to sit and look out over the ocean.'

So they sat, and for some reason, before long, they held hands.

It was comfortable, and companionable, and although he knew he must be wrong to be thinking this way, it seemed to Tom, after a while, that it might almost be better than sex...

Then he remembered the kiss they'd shared in the rainforest and knew he was probably wrong...

CHAPTER SIX

TOM'S new, unprecedented reactions to Lauren needed thought, while the effect her presence in his house was having on him required a lot of consideration. He took both the thought and the further consideration with him when he went to bed. They'd sat for an hour, maybe a little more, desultory conversation starting and stopping between them, nothing startling, nothing even important, catching up on each other's recent lives, discussing all the little things about bringing up a child that neither of them had ever considered.

'Not that he's ours,' Lauren had said, and he'd caught a note of not sadness but definitely regret in her voice.

'No, he couldn't be,' Tom had told her, and felt the same regret inside him.

Not that he wanted an eight-year-old boy.

Not that he wanted a child of any kind.

Children needed commitment.

Children needed love...

He stopped thinking about Bobby and children in general and definitely stopped thinking about love, eventually drifting off to sleep, thinking about a woman in a bed two rooms away...

Not that sleep lasted long, the jangling summons of the phone bringing him into a sitting position to answer it—something he'd trained himself to do after he'd learned that answering the phone lying down meant risking going back to sleep.

Lauren met him in the passage as he pulled on his shirt before hurrying across to the hospital.

'Accident?' she asked.

Tom nodded, then touched her on the shoulder.

'I'm sorry the phone woke you. Go back to bed. I could be a while.'

'Good luck,' she whispered, and now he understood why he'd felt not lonely but a little strange lying in his big bed earlier—he was becoming accustomed to having Lauren in his house, having someone who cared about him enough to pour him coffee, eat meals with, or say good luck when he went out into the night to face the terrible things people could do to themselves or others.

'Thanks,' he said, and bent to kiss her, aiming for her cheek, changing his mind at the last moment because the kiss that had somehow happened near the waterfall had tasted sweet and clean, and he wanted to check the taste again, to feel the softness of those lips, trembling just slightly beneath his.

He left the house with the taste of her on his tongue and an image of her in his head—standing in his house in a very short nightshirt covered with fat angels of some kind. Had she stiffened when he'd kissed her?

Her lips had responded, as they had earlier, but earlier she'd definitely pushed away, and this time...

A paramedic from the ambulance was wheeling a gurney into the ER when Tom reached the hospital. On it, hooked up to monitors and oxygen, was a young woman with dark hair—vaguely familiar, although Tom couldn't say how he knew her.

The marks on her neck were vivid red welts and she lay carefully still, as if other parts of her body were hurting.

'What do we know?' he asked the paramedic.

The man turned to him, shock on his face.

'It's Mrs Williams, Nat Williams's wife. His mother phoned for us.'

'Police?'

'Nat's mother said she wanted to but Mrs Williams said no.'

'It's assault—we have to report it,' Tom said, but he was already bent over the woman, checking the readouts from the monitors, taking in all he could of her outward appearance, lifting her hair and feeling her skull for irregularities, thinking about the damage strangulation could do to the airway, spinal cord and blood vessels within the unprotected structure of the human neck.

'I'm Tom Fletcher, a doctor,' he said, but the woman on the gurney didn't respond, a blank look in her eyes telling Tom she either didn't hear or couldn't comprehend.

Blood vessels could be occluded in strangling, blocked arteries causing lack of oxygen to the brain, blocked veins causing increased pressure— so many dangerous possibilities.

'She spoke to you?' he asked the paramedic.

'Just to whisper no when the older Mrs Williams said she was calling the police.'

Tom signed the transfer papers, then read quickly

through his copy, checking all that had been done for the woman so far.

She had an oxygen mask on her face but no intubation. Mrs Williams was breathing so apparently her airway wasn't severely compromised. In such cases, endotracheal intubation wouldn't have been attempted in the field...

His mind raced through what he knew of strangulation injuries—the airway could swell later and intubation become necessary with little warning. She had an oximeter on one finger and her blood oxyhaemoglobin was good—he didn't need an arterial blood gas test right now.

Laryngeal fracture was possible, he'd need to do a CT scan of the neck and probably the head, although the first thing to do was make her comfortable.

He set down the papers and began his own examination, speaking quietly to her as he turned her head to examine the bruising, feeling her skull for any other damage, calling for the portable X-ray machine so they could check her here without moving her again.

'Can you hear me?'

She nodded.

'Can you talk?'

A whispered 'No', so weak and shaky Tom regretted asking her, especially as she was crying now, silent tears sliding down her cheeks.

He touched her shoulder.

'It's okay, we'll look after you. Just nod or shake your head to answer, but don't shake hard, okay?'

He wiped the tears away, patting her cheek gently at the same time.

'Are you hurting anywhere else?'

A nod.

'Your head?'

A shake.

'We'll work our way down,' Tom told her. 'Shoulders?'

A nod and her left hand lifted to point to her right shoulder.

He should have seen it earlier, but she was so thin her bones stuck out everywhere, the knot where a broken bone had healed masking the dislocation.

'Your shoulder has popped out of its socket,' he told her. 'Easy to fix. I could give you a fast-acting general anaesthetic but don't want too much fluid running into you right now so I'll use a couple of local anaesthetics to numb the area around the joint and pop it back in.'

He was doing his best to sound casual about the situation, not wanting to inflict more fear on her—especially fear of more pain.

'I need to X-ray it but I'll give you the injections first so they can be working while we do the X-rays.'

The machine was wheeled into place as he injected the local anaesthetic, then he helped her into a sitting position, feeling her wince and knowing she was probably hurting all over but being as gentle as he could. One of the nursing staff was an excellent radiography technician and fortunately she was on duty, taking the shots he needed with minimum fuss.

Tom called another nurse in to hold Mrs Williams in a sitting position while he checked the negatives, realising he'd need to do another X-ray once he'd manoeuvred the joint back into position—then later a CT scan for ligament damage—thinking all the time, blocking the thought of how the injuries might have occurred from his mind with what needed doing right now.

Blocking the thought of Lauren from his mind as

well, refusing to think about her uncharacteristic reaction to Nat Williams.

The ball slid into place in the socket, and a second series of X-rays confirmed it was in place. He held his patient's arm in position against her chest and helped her to lie down again.

'Later on, I'll put your arm into a sling to keep the shoulder stable and you'll need to keep it as immobile as you can until the swelling and inflammation around the joint subside.'

She nodded, her eyes almost closed. The anaesthetic, pain and shock would be making her feel incredibly weary, but Tom knew he had to complete his examination—already interrupted to ease her pain—although if her airway remained unimpaired he could leave the scans until the next day when there'd be a radiographer on duty and specialists available in Port. He could send the scans over the internet to the experts if there was anything worrying on them.

Still talking to her, he lowered the sheet that covered her, not entirely surprised to see that she was naked beneath it—not entirely surprised to see the yellowish marks of old bruising on her breasts. People used near-strangulation in erotic sex games and if she didn't want the police involved it could be she was a willing participant.

In which case shouldn't her husband have accompanied her to the hospital?

Her husband, Nat Williams, the man Lauren… feared?

No, too big a leap to make, concentrate on the patient. Alyssa Williams. He called her by her name when he spoke to her this time but she was beyond responding, not unconscious but sleeping.

He completed his examination, almost certain she couldn't have been a willing participant in whatever sex she'd endured when he saw the bruising on her inner thighs. Yet another instance of the destructive forces of love, he told himself, sickened by the woman's injuries, angry that a man could get away with such things because his victim refused to seek help…

He left two nurses to carefully collect the evidence needed for a rape kit, explaining that it might not be needed but wanting the evidence kept anyway, reminding them to take photos, apologising to Alyssa for the intrusion. Once that was done, they would clean her carefully and dress her in a hospital gown, women helping another woman in trouble, gentle hands and soft voices.

He cursed softly to himself as he wrote up his notes, aware all the time of tension deep inside him, tension not entirely connected to his patient. Part of it was, of course, the tension he always felt when he saw the damage men could inflict on women.

The other part was personal and the cursing was because he'd never mixed his personal and professional lives, yet now he couldn't help but feel a niggling suspicion, not to mention a deep, fierce anger, that the same man might once have harmed Lauren!

It's all supposition, he reminded himself, dragging his mind firmly back to the patient in question.

'Is there a private room free?' he asked one of the nurses.

'There's that room near the veranda. The woman from the stands' accident went home this afternoon,' the nurse replied.

'Let's take Mrs Williams there,' he said, then, although he knew it was probably useless to remind them of patient confidentiality, he did point out that if word about this got around town her husband might see to it that she suffered even more.

'And none of us would like that on our consciences,' he reminded the two women.

They nodded, both of them, he guessed, as affected by the woman's injuries as he was, and probably more horrified by who had inflicted them—after all the nurses were locals and had probably known Nat Williams in the past.

Like Lauren?

No, the nurses were both older, so hardly likely to have gone out with him, and the patient confidentiality he'd just spoken of applied to him as well so he could hardly question Lauren about her relationship with Nat…

'I'll stay with her,' he said, when they'd settled Alyssa in the bedroom. 'I'm a little worried about her airway and would rather be on hand if anything goes wrong.'

He sat beside the woman and dozed a little in the chair, waking as the sky lightened across the ocean, and the details of the little town started becoming clearer, lights dimming and finally disappearing as the sun rose and proclaimed a fresh, new day.

Fresh? He felt like death warmed up and it wasn't only tiredness dogging him.

'Phone, Tom.'

He took the handpiece and walked out onto the veranda before answering.

'This is Karen Williams, Nat's mother, Alyssa's mother-in-law. How is she?'

'She's resting, Mrs Williams. She'll be all right.'

'She won't be all right,' the forthright woman declared. 'Not if she goes back to him. I can't believe my own son—but, still, he's not your worry. Can you talk her into going to the police? She'll say he was drunk, he didn't mean it, but he's got to be stopped, do you know what I mean?'

'I do, Mrs Williams, and while I agree, I believe it's up to Alyssa to make the complaint. The children, are they all right?'

'I'll make darned sure they are and that they stay all right, you can tell her that, and she can come home here as soon as she's ready, because he won't be staying here, no matter how big a local hero he thinks he is.'

Tom assured her he'd pass the message on, and returned to Alyssa's room to find her awake, staring at the ceiling, the blankness in her eyes disturbing him more than the very visible bruising on her neck.

'That was your mother-in-law on the phone. She said to tell you the kids are fine and that she'd welcome you home any time. She wanted to assure you Nat wouldn't be there.'

Tom sat down by the bed and took Alyssa's hand.

'She also thinks you should report him to the police.'

Alyssa shook her head, so tiredly Tom knew she'd been told this before and had probably argued it out with herself many, many times, for some reason always coming up with an excuse to protect the man who battered her.

Love?

'I know something of domestic violence,' Tom told her, while his head was scoffing at the 'love' question. He might not know much about love but he knew for sure it didn't inflict pain on the loved one. 'I'm on the board of the local refuge. If you want to talk about it to someone who understands...'

He was about to mention Lauren when his own suspicions stopped him, although Lauren was definitely the person he should bring in.

'It's only when he drinks, and maybe does a line of coke,' Alyssa said.

Tom put the two drugs together in his mind. Coaethylene—more toxic than either drug on its own—caused heart problems not to mention liver toxicity, and the combination accentuated the effect of both drugs.

He wondered just how long Alyssa could go on making excuses for her husband, listening to his words of love, empty words, accepting gestures of love, expensive gifts, believing he loved her because she wanted, perhaps needed to believe?

Until he killed her?

Anger at the man pounded through Tom's body.

He wondered, too, about his reaction. He'd seen evidence of domestic abuse before, too many times, but had never felt the strong surge of impotent rage that he was feeling now…

Yet in spite of the rage and whatever the cause of it—more than Alyssa's injuries?—he had to bring Lauren in on the case.

Time to get his head straight!

He left Alyssa in the care of a nurse, asking that someone stay with her at all times, and walked across to his house, drinking in the quiet of the early morning, allowing it to soothe his warring feelings.

Quiet until he entered the front door and heard the argument going on in the kitchen.

Smelt the smoke.

'Paper doesn't get into a toaster by accident, Bobby, and you know it. Dr Tom's being good enough to let us stay here and you want to thank him by setting fire to his house?'

The strain in Lauren's voice suggested this wasn't the first time she'd remonstrated with the child they'd promised to protect.

'Didn't set it on fire,' came the sullen reply. 'Bit of smoke, that's all.'

'A bit of smoke that ruined the toaster,' Lauren pointed out, at which stage Tom considered his options. One—go quietly back to the hospital and try to find a bed there to snatch a couple of hours' badly needed sleep. Two—see if he could sneak into his bedroom without them hearing, and attempt to sleep there. Or, three, join the pair in the kitchen, perhaps acting as jury to the judge and accused.

At least the prospect of entering the kitchen had diverted his anger!

He called out a slightly forced 'Good morning' and proceeded to the kitchen, where Lauren's pathetically grateful smile more than made up for Bobby's scowling countenance.

'Little mishap?' Tom queried, winking at Lauren to let her know he'd heard the basics.

'It was nothin',' Bobby told him. 'She's fussing 'bout nothin'.'

'I'm not fussing, Bobby,' Lauren said, so gently Tom wondered at her patience. 'I'm just asking you not to do silly things that might injure you or damage Tom's property. Okay?'

Bobby glared at her, and recognising an impasse when he saw one Tom stepped in again.

'Let's all go down the road for breakfast,' he suggested, although he was so tired and mentally confused he wanted nothing more than to escape into his bedroom. 'We can eat, then, if you want to go to school, we can drop you off, or if you don't want to go to school, you and Lauren can make plans for the day. Okay?'

Bobby frowned at him.

'You're not angry?' he finally demanded.

'Angry about what?' Tom asked.

The little boy shuffled awkwardly, then looked

up at Tom, his dark eyes holding a plea—for understanding?

Or simple affection?

'I bust your toaster,' he said.

'Oh, that's okay,' Tom told him. 'We can buy another one. Just as long as you don't do it again or set fire to the house, we'll be okay.'

Bobby beamed at him, then shot Lauren a look that said, See, he's not upset, far more clearly than words ever would have.

Lauren accepted it with good grace, smiling at Bobby and ruffling his hair.

'Come on, then, let's go.' She turned to Tom. 'We talked about school and Bobby's decided not to go. We're going to go shopping for some boots he can wear at the farm when we go out after Christmas, and some new jeans in case he wants to go riding—'

'And a checked shirt and a cowboy hat,' Bobby finished for her.

He scooted off to his room and Lauren looked at Tom, reading the exhaustion in his face but so grateful for the way he'd handled the situation she wanted to hug him.

Again!

'Thanks,' she said instead. 'I realise it's the last thing you want to do but we'll eat quickly.'

Tom ignored her gratitude, instead lifting the eyebrow that she so envied as he said, 'Cowboy hat?'

Lauren grimaced.

'I know! I tried to explain it wasn't exactly the wild west, our family farm, but he has this image in his head and I can't get rid of it. Still, he'll need a hat so it might as well be a cowboy hat.'

'And what was he burning in the toaster?' Tom asked, and Lauren had to frown.

'I've no idea. I didn't think of that—I was just so upset to see the flames shooting out of the thing...'

She crossed the room and opened the back door, retrieving the ruined toaster from the veranda railing, fishing inside it with her finger, pulling out a corner of paper that had escaped incineration.

'A photo perhaps?' she said, bringing it across to show to Tom, but as Bobby had reappeared, an ancient wallet clasped in one hand, Tom slipped the scrap into his pocket and the conversation ended there, while the conversation he knew he had to have about Alyssa hadn't even started.

Bobby was their immediate priority, he told himself, and Alyssa was having further tests and then would need to rest. If Lauren could see her this afternoon...

If...

Their breakfast was surprisingly enjoyable and Lauren realised that it was because Bobby was relating well to Tom, accepting his word that wholegrain bread made men stronger than white bread so the little boy ordered wholegrain toast, and generally following Tom's lead in both ordering his breakfast and then in the order of eating it—finishing eggs before they tackled bacon, finishing that before they ate their beans.

'I can never understand why some people do that,' Lauren finally declared. 'It's the taste of bacon and beans and egg all together that makes breakfast such a good meal.'

Tom smiled at her and although it was a weary effort, it lit the coils of heat again and she had to sternly admonish herself that this was work, not playtime. Well, kind of work!

'I like things to taste of what they are,' Tom told her, then he winked—second time this morning—and she felt a shiver run through her, as if the wink had somehow made the simple statement naughty.

'Me too,' Bobby declared, and Lauren laughed, aware the little boy who needed someone special in his life had found himself a hero.

They left the café, Tom admonishing Bobby to be good for Lauren, Lauren telling Tom to make sure he went home to get some sleep.

'And don't detour via the hospital,' she added, as Bobby wandered off to look in a toyshop window. 'You know they'll call you if they need you.'

Tom hesitated on the footpath, his face serious— frowning, in fact, drawing her slightly away from Bobby.

'I've got to detour via the hospital to check some scans and, later, I need to talk to you,' he said, very quietly. 'I need you to see someone, if not today then tomorrow.'

Lauren frowned right back at him.

'You sound as if you're forcing those words out against your will. You ask me to see people all the time—well, not *all* the time, but often enough, so what's different?'

Before he could reply, Bobby disappeared into the toyshop and with a hurried 'Sorry! We'll talk later,' Lauren rushed after him.

But the strained uncertainty on Tom's face bothered her.

Perhaps it was just tiredness.

She caught up with Bobby as he began to take a display of plastic animals apart, but it was Jo who stopped the destruction.

'What are you doing here?' Lauren demanded, unable to believe her previously workaholic friend was in a shop on a Monday morning.

'I'm the designated shopper for the refuge, remember,' Jo replied, detaching Bobby from a seriously large rocket ship at the same time. 'And now I've got an employee I can take time off now and then.'

Lauren smiled automatically, how could she not when her best friend was practically glowing with happiness? But then another image, Tom's worried face, the shadows in his eyes, flashed across Lauren's mind.

'Great!' she said to Jo as a solution occurred to her. 'How about you ask Bobby to help you choose the toys? I really need to talk to Tom about something.'

Jo frowned at her—everyone was doing it!

'I won't be long,' Lauren added, all but tripping

over the words because suddenly it seemed she *had* to know what was worrying Tom. 'Bobby knows the kids in the refuge at the moment and he'll know what they want. Maybe shop then have an ice cream in the park. He's fine as long as he's eating. Phone me if you have a problem, and I'll be at the hospital or Tom's house when you finish.'

She turned to Bobby, who was only too pleased to be able to spend longer in the toyshop, although he did extract a promise from Lauren that they'd get the cowboy hat later.

Jo raised her eyebrows at the mention of the cowboy hat.

'I'll explain some other time,' Lauren promised, then, because she felt she was somehow letting him down, she gave Bobby a hug and a quick kiss on the cheek, refrained from telling him to be good, and hurried up the hill to the hospital.

Tom was in his office, frowning again, but this time at some X-rays he had up in the light box, but his face lightened as she knocked briefly and walked in, and she felt a rush of pleasure that she could change his mood.

Or maybe it wasn't her—maybe he'd just needed a distraction…

'You've killed our kid?' he joked.

'Jo's got him buying toys,' Lauren explained. 'You looked worried when you said you wanted to see me so I thought I'd come up while I had the chance.'

Where to begin?

And did he really want to discuss this with her?

Tom studied the beautiful face of the woman opposite him. Yes, she was concerned—of course she would be, having picked up on his concern earlier—but the smile she'd flashed as she'd talked of Bobby still lingered on her face and he was ninety-nine per cent certain he was going to wipe that smile away and probably replace the questions in her eyes with dark, unfathomable shadows…

'Jo won't keep him all day!' the beautiful woman prompted, and Tom sighed, then came around from behind his desk, took Lauren's hand, and led her to the small couch beside a coffee table that he considered the informal section of his office.

He sat down, drawing her down beside him, still unable to find the words he needed, so in the end he blurted out the one question he probably shouldn't have asked.

Blurted it right out!

'Did Nat Williams abuse you?'

Instant regret as she turned pale beneath her golden tan, and her fingers tightened so hard on his he felt a stab of physical pain as well as the internal jolt he'd earned from hurting her.

'Why do you ask?'

He heard the quiver in her usually placid voice, and felt her fingers grip tighter, then, while he watched, she detached herself both mentally and physically, straightening up, breathing deeply, letting go of his hand and moving a little away from him on the couch.

Hazel eyes scanned his face, so intensely focussed he knew she'd see any hint of him dissembling.

'The admission last night—or early this morning—was Alyssa Williams.'

Lauren's reaction was immediate.

'Was she strangled?'

Tom was too shocked to reply but his face must have answered for him.

'Dear Heaven! What have I done?' she cried, springing to her feet and pacing back and forth in front of him, muttering more to herself than to him, wringing her hands in such an agitated manner he wondered if he should attempt to hold her, calm her.

Or would a man's touch be too hateful to her right now as bad memories flooded her head?

Before he could decide, she was speaking again.

'I should have said, should have spoken out, told someone, anyone. Maybe he could have been stopped and who knows how many women he's hurt since then? Women I could have saved if I'd only said something.'

Her voice was becoming strident, regret, fear, guilt and memories melding together to throw the usually controlled woman he knew close to panic. Thrusting aside any doubts, he stood up and caught her as she paced, holding her hard against his body, talking, talking, talking...

'You're a professional,' he reminded her. 'How old were you anyway? Had you even heard of this kind of abuse? Who would you have told?'

He held her close, feeling the emotion that shook her body, while anger grew again inside him.

Anger solved nothing, he reminded himself, but how else to react to Lauren's gut-wrenching sobs as the walls she'd erected around the past shattered into sharp, destructive shards?

He let her cry, talking, reassuring, unaware most of the time of what he was saying, simply letting words fill the air in the hope they might help, and maybe they did for she finally eased away from him, not abruptly, but gently, and this time *he* took his handkerchief from his pocket and handed it to her.

She dried her eyes and slumped back onto the couch, pouring herself a glass of water from the carafe he kept there, sipping at it, eyes downcast, breathing deeply again. He sat beside her, not too close, concerned for her and uncertain how to show it, aching for her but knowing he couldn't show his own emotion.

Earlier he'd known a hug was needed but now?

'I'm sorry,' she said, finally turning to face him and resting her hand on his knee. 'I had no idea all that was going to come boiling out, but I've lived with guilt over what happened for so long...'

'Guilt? Why should *you* feel guilt? Guilt's your emotion talking, not your brain!'

He couldn't help it—the words just bulldozed their way out, tight with suppressed anger at the man who'd hurt her, not at Lauren.

Her touch firmed on his knee and she actually

found a smile—a small, feeble effort but still a smile.

Silence rested between them, not entirely easy, but he guessed she was finding the words she wanted, perhaps needed, to say, so he rested his hand on hers and told himself to keep his mouth shut.

And ignore the ache that still filled his chest...

'It wasn't guilt at first,' she finally began, hesitantly producing the words. 'It was shame.'

The memory coloured her cheeks and he had to remind himself he was there to listen, not to take her in his arms again.

'Terrible shame because I thought it was my fault, or that it always happened with sex and I was just too stupid to know.'

She looked up at him then, her eyes enormous in her pale face, the pathetic smile wobbling slightly.

'Stupid, isn't it? All the study I've done since, all the women I've met and talked to and counselled and advised since then, and yet my own past has the power to affect me like this—to turn me back into my sixteen-year-old self who was so overawed that someone like Nat Williams could like me, I'm a quivering mess just thinking about it! Not only that, but I'm still blaming myself for what he did—taking the 'it must have been my fault' line like every abused woman I've ever met, although some of the guilt is probably more to do with not telling, but at the time, well, I had no idea it shouldn't be like that and it was so awful, so truly horrible, I couldn't even talk to Jo, my best friend, about it, let alone my mother, or Jo's dad, who was our doctor. I thought he loved me—thought maybe it was normal. I kept thinking—what if that's what sex is all about? I guess the only thing that I did do right was to stop seeing him, or maybe I wasn't even strong enough to do that—maybe he went off to a competition somewhere and that was that. I can't even remember that part, only the—'

She broke off so abruptly Tom forgot about being there to listen. Anyway, he could listen with her in his arms. He moved so he could hold her once again, wrapping his arms around her, bringing her body against his when she relaxed into his grasp and leant against him, the air and the words that had floated on it going out of her with the suddenness of a pricked balloon.

Tom held her, not talking now, not wanting to talk, but his mind raced along tangled paths that became clearer as all she'd said slotted into what he knew of Lauren. Her empathy with battered women came from deeper down than study, while her detachment—in particular, her avoidance of relationships with men—had grown from an experience of something that should have been passable at least, good, or even wonderful at best, but had been horrifying and painful and—

He couldn't think about it, simply tightening his arms around her and holding her for as long as she needed to be held, comforting her, reassuring her.

Just holding her…

For ever?

Now, where had that thought come from?

Not for ever, just several minutes, then the Lauren he knew returned, smiling at him, a better effort this time, mopping at her face with her handkerchief once again then leaning over to kiss him quickly on the lips.

'Thank you,' she said, simple words but he knew they were heartfelt. 'You need to grab some sleep and I need to rescue Jo from Bobby, but I'm okay now and I'll definitely see Alyssa whenever you think she's ready for a visit.'

She hesitated, cocking her head to one side and

studying him before adding, 'I'm okay, Tom, I really am. I guess all that stuff had to come out, but I can be totally professional with Alyssa, please don't doubt that.'

Tom thought his heart might break, so badly did it hurt just listening to Lauren's assurances, which he knew covered the fragility she must be feeling. He cupped her head with the palms of his hands and looked deep into her eyes.

'Of course you'll be professional—I never for a second doubted that!' he managed, but the words were gruff, roughly spoken, blurted out because he wanted to do so much more for her but had no idea how to begin to help her or even if she needed, or would want, his help.

But he had to try.

'And being a professional you must know that regrets are wasted. Do you really think you might have stopped him—Nat Williams, king of the Aussie surfing world, a testosterone-filled young man who thought he was God?'

He pressed his lips to hers, very gently, before adding, firm now, authoritative, 'None of this is your fault, Lauren, none of it, and you'd better believe that!'

And he kissed her again—just a kiss—a friend's kiss with maybe a hint of the would-be lover in it so she'd know the man who'd kissed her by the waterfall—the man she'd definitely kissed back—was still there for her...

And *that* thought hurt his heart again...

CHAPTER SEVEN

I REALLY have to stop crying all over Tom!

Lauren shook her head as the random thought echoed in her brain. Of all the things to be thinking!

It was obviously a symptom of her shattered state and her state *was* shattered, her insides like mush for all she was pretending everything was okay.

Perhaps thinking about crying against Tom's chest was her brain's way of avoiding what she should be thinking about—although thinking about the past and in particular her past with Nat was hardly going to achieve anything right now.

She shivered in the summer sunshine as she hurried down the road, glad she had a job ahead of her—shopping with Bobby—knowing later she'd have to sit down and have a proper think—about the past, about professionalism and Alyssa

Williams, and probably about what poor Tom must be thinking of his houseguest right now.

He was right, of course, about her rushing into words when she was anxious or confused, but to have rushed all those words out to him—to Tom of all people.

Her mind balked and she knew it was because of the way she'd been feeling about Tom lately— about the stupid coils of heat—and now he knew about her past, about Nat Williams, well, the heat-coiling stuff should stop right now because Tom was probably...

Probably what?

As if she had a clue how anyone would react to revelations of past abuse, let alone how Tom might react! If anything, given his experience with the refuge, he'd probably be more understanding than most, but when she'd tried, that one time, to explain to a then boyfriend why the idea of sex terrified her—

She blanked that memory out and turned her mind to Bobby. His welfare was far more impor-tant than her attraction to her host.

She'd concentrate on Bobby.

'You've been a long time.' Bobby's accusatory

glare was rather spoiled by the fact that the words were spoken around a double ice-cream cone. 'We've been waiting for ages!'

'At least three minutes,' Jo added, though Lauren sensed relief in the words.

'Trouble?' she queried quietly, while Bobby chased a pigeon off a park bench.

'Not really,' Jo assured her, 'but he's certainly a full-attention job.'

She paused, peering closely at her friend.

'Bad news? Had Tom heard from Children's Services?'

Lauren shook her head.

'I'm the bad news,' she muttered, shaking her head as she remembered her total meltdown. 'But I'm okay now or I will be soon and one day I promise I'll explain, just not today.'

Jo knew her well enough not to push, contenting herself with a kiss on Lauren's cheek and a quick shoulder squeeze before chasing Bobby around the park bench, threatening to kiss him.

'No sloppy kisses!' he said, standing at bay, then, to Lauren's delight, he added in a very embarrassed mutter, 'Except for Lauren.'

The past didn't exactly vanish but the day grew

brighter and she bent to hug the little boy, thanking Jo for minding him and promising to get together soon.

'Now we can buy the cowboy hat?' Bobby asked, and she had to laugh at his persistence. The past would definitely have to go back into its box for a while. As Jo had said, Bobby was a full-attention job!

'*Now* we'll buy the cowboy hat,' she agreed, and hand in hand they walked down the road to the clothing shop, Lauren hoping that taking Bobby shopping would be challenging enough to blank the past from her mind, for a while, at least.

He soon proved he was up to the challenge. Tact, that's what was needed, tact and patience. But as she discussed his choice of clothing, she couldn't help but remember her own behaviour when she'd shopped as a child with her mother, always wanting something too extreme, too trendy, too poor in quality to last.

Who had shopped with Tom?

The grandmother?

Foster-mother?

Some well-meaning woman from Children's Services?

Tom!

What must he be thinking of her? Dumping all that angst on him like some hysterical teenager…

'This shirt?' Bobby was holding up a shirt with tassels on the pockets, Western style. Lauren brought her attention back to the boy she was with, tucking all thoughts of Tom—boy and man—away in the back of her mind.

'But I'm a growing boy.' This was Bobby's next protest when, having agreed to the tasselled shirt, she stood firm and bought the jeans that fitted him, not the pair with fancy studs and stitching that were two sizes too large.

'We'll buy you new ones when you grow,' Lauren promised him, then heard her own words and hoped that someone, if it wasn't her, would keep her promise to the child.

She paid for their purchases and led him out of the shop, keeping to the shade as they walked up the hill to the hospital and the sheltering house beside it.

Tom managed to grab an hour's sleep, and woke, if not full of energy, at least refreshed. The house was quiet so he assumed his guests were still shopping.

A long, hot shower, shaving under the hot water, refreshed him enough to dress then phone the hospital, pleased to hear that the full-body scan he'd ordered for Alyssa Williams had been carried out and the film sent through to a radiologist in Port Macquarie, the large regional town down the road.

'We're waiting to hear the results but Mrs Williams wants to go home,' Tom's colleague told him. 'What do you think?'

'Definitely not until we hear the radiologist's report. I'm concerned about oedema in her head, damage to her larynx, torn ligaments around her shoulder and other internal soft-tissue damage. She's also pregnant, which complicates things. Keep reassuring her the children are okay—their grandmother is looking after them.'

'Are you reporting it?'

Not until I've discussed it with Lauren, he thought but didn't say, then wondered if his hesitation was because of Lauren or his patient.

'Not yet. I've asked Lauren to talk to Alyssa later today, when she's feeling up to a visit,' he explained, assuring himself it was Alyssa's well-being in the forefront of his mind.

The question of reporting it haunted Tom. Reporting it would bring in a whole raft of outsiders—Lauren among them—but starting with the police. They would question Alyssa, talk to her about the options she had, advise and consult, and generally attempt to help her out of the situation in which she found herself.

A situation she might not want to escape no matter how sensible escape would be.

His stomach clenched at the thought of what battered women went through both physically and emotionally or maybe clenched at the thought of what the teenage Lauren had suffered, but his stomach would just have to live with it.

'Alyssa's emotionally fragile,' he continued to explain to his colleague. 'And right now she's also a long way from her own family and friends so she's lacking support, although her mother-in-law is behind her and all for reporting it. I'm concerned that pushing her into the system might make things much harder for her. Let's leave it until Lauren's seen her.'

He ended the conversation, promising he'd be

over at the hospital before long, then sat down on the veranda to try to sort out the increasingly twisted strands of thought inside his head.

Ignoring the strand that was Lauren, he considered how Alyssa must be feeling. She was American so being out here in Australia might mean she was cut off from her family and friends. But he knew enough about DV situations to know the woman was nearly always isolated from her support very early on in the relationship.

Tom looked hopefully down the drive. Lauren would know what to do.

Was he being fair, asking this of her?

Oh, she'd handle it, for all the emotional storm she'd suffered earlier. The professional Lauren he knew could handle anything, but at what risk to the woman inside her professional armour?

Realising that his thoughts were becoming more tangled than ever, he gave up trying to sort the muddle and returned to the hospital.

Lauren and Bobby walked slowly home. The house was quiet but the door to Tom's room was open, the bed unmade but empty.

'He must have gone back to work,' she said to

Bobby, but he was far too excited unpacking his new clothes to worry about his protector, while Lauren was relieved to find she could avoid the man for a little longer, her embarrassment over her meltdown still burning in her, while guilt still nibbled around the edges of her mind.

Fortunately she had Bobby as a diversion—a very good diversion as it happened when he unpacked his new clothes and announced, 'I'll put them on now and ride the bike over to the house to show the other kids.'

Lauren wanted to protest that they needed to be washed first, but his face was shiny with excitement and she couldn't dampen it. Although riding over to the house? It was only a couple of blocks, but how old should kids be before they were allowed to ride bikes around town on their own?

She'd been driving the old ute on the farm when she wasn't much older than Bobby but, never having lived in town, she wasn't certain of the 'rules'!

'I could drive you over,' she suggested, thinking about time and when Alyssa might be well enough for a visit. Her mind was swinging between Bobby and the patient while she resolutely ignored any thoughts of the past. 'I can put the bike in my car and you can ride it around the yard when we get to the house, although most of the kids will still be at school. So what if we do this?'

Bobby offered her a suspicious glare, the shiny excitement gone, and she knew she had to put him first—at least until Tom could take over the child-care or she could get Jo back to babysit.

'What?'

'We wash your new clothes because sometimes new clothes are stiff and prickly and washing will make them soft, and by the time we've put them through the dryer, the kids at the house will be home from school and you can show them then.'

'So what'll I do now?' her small guest demanded.

Watching another of the hospital DVDs would be the ideal solution, but Lauren was sure that too much TV was bad for children.

'How about you help me work out how to use Dr Tom's washing machine? Mine's different but you're a boy so you should be able to work it out for me.'

Blatant sexism in that statement but she knew she had to keep him occupied, though getting the washing machine started wouldn't take for ever…

'Get any other dirty clothes you've got out of your bedroom,' she told him, and though he balked he did go off, muttering to himself, returning with what must be the entire contents of his small duffel bag.

'It's all dirty,' he announced. 'Mum hated washing.'

'I don't think anyone loves it,' Lauren told him. 'But with machines it's a lot easier. My old granny used to boil all the clothes in a copper. It was outside the house, and you had to light a fire under it, and carry the water to it in buckets.'

'Like a witch's cauldron? The thing witches put stuff in to make spells?' Bobby asked, and as Lauren acknowledged the old coppers were very like a witch's cauldron, she wondered if he'd seen such things on television or a DVD or if he was a reader.

She hoped it was the latter and made a mental note to collect some more books that might suit him from the refuge.

The refuge!

She'd had so much on her mind since Friday she hadn't even collected the cheque from the fundraising. Would it be enough to keep the refuge open?

For a short time at least…

Should she be concentrating on that rather than an orphaned little boy?

Of course not! Right now Bobby needed her, and later Alyssa needed her, and later again—well, then she'd think about the refuge…

The boy who needed her most was in the laundry, carefully studying all the knobs on the washing machine, eventually telling Lauren they should look for a book of instructions.

'Not because I can't work it,' he assured her, 'but we don't want to bust Tom's washing machine.'

Tom, not Dr Tom—well that was okay, Lauren decided. Tom had moved from the professional Bobby might have seen at the hospital where he was Dr Tom to everyone, to a protector.

A friend?

Lauren hoped so.

She found the washing machine manual on a shelf above the machine and wondered for a moment where someone coming into her house might find hers—in a box under the bed perhaps?

In with her recipe books in a basket in the kitchen?

Turning her mind back to Bobby, she found him studying the illustrations and comparing them to the machine, taking total responsibility for the operation. He set all the buttons and dials and got it going, Lauren crossing her fingers behind her back that it would work because he was refusing to allow her to look at the book.

'It will take forty-eight minutes,' he announced, closing the book but keeping hold of it. 'What can we do for forty-eight minutes?'

Have a reasonably good panic attack, was Lauren's first thought but she forced the past—and what lay ahead—from her mind again.

'Have lunch? I know it's late but we had a late breakfast and you had ice cream with Jo but we should have something to eat. And we should do some grocery shopping while we're out, so we're not eating all Tom's food. We'll make sandwiches and while we're eating we'll write a shopping list. You can tell me what you like to eat.'

'Sausages,' Bobby announced, 'and Tom's got a barbecue, I saw it outside on the veranda. I like barbecued sausages in bread with tomato sauce, only I like ordinary sausages best, not the fancy ones like we got at the markets yesterday. They were okay but I like shop sausages best.'

Thinking of sausages was a sure cure for panic attacks!

The market sausages were probably healthier, but however much he liked sausages of any kind, Lauren doubted they were nutritious food for a growing boy—not if eaten every day. She thought about this as Bobby opened Tom's pantry and surveyed the spreads available for sandwiches, announcing he'd have peanut butter.

'And he hasn't got any cereal, so you'd better put that on the list,' he added. 'I like Frosty Flakes, the kind with the gorilla on the packet.'

Lauren had never heard of Frosty Flakes let alone seen a gorilla on a packet of cereal but she found a pen and paper and obediently wrote Frosty Flakes on it, adding milk, which would surely be needed to go with the cereal.

And sausages in case he really wouldn't eat anything else.

And bread.

And tomato sauce…

Later she'd have a think about nutrition but right

now it seemed a good idea to have food in the house that Bobby would actually eat.

Caring for a growing boy, as Bobby had called himself, was certainly throwing up some challenges...

Bobby was on his fourth peanut-butter sandwich—when to stop, something else she'd have to check—when Tom walked in. Lauren's stomach squelched and embarrassment flooded her body, but Tom's easy grin restored a little of her equilibrium, enough for her to ask, 'Peanut-butter sandwich?' as casually as if she hadn't been weeping all over him only a couple of hours earlier.

'Thanks,' Tom said, his grin turning into an 'everything's okay' kind of smile just for her, the message in his eyes telling her they'd get through this, although what Tom had to get through she didn't know...

He ruffled Bobby's hair as he walked past to subside into a chair beside the young boy, who, Lauren noticed, moved in his chair, just a little closer to Tom.

Fair enough, she could have done with being closer to Tom herself, so confused did she feel.

Not that she could rely on him to sort her out. He was a friend, nothing more.

'Coffee or tea?' she offered, dragging her attention back to her housewifely duties, passing him a sandwich.

'Coffee would be lovely but you don't have to get it.'

She smiled at him, a real smile this time, as Tom's remembered kindness while she'd stuttered out her confession warmed the cold and shaken bits inside her.

'That protest lacks oomph,' she teased him. 'To make it really effective you have to pretend to be getting up from the chair, probably groaning a little with the effort.'

He smiled back at her and for a moment she felt a stillness in the air, the room disappearing from in front of her eyes—as if some cataclysmic change was occurring.

Surely not from a smile.

It was a hangover reaction from earlier.

Although…

Steadying herself, she boiled the electric kettle and poured the water over coffee grounds in Tom's plunger, mentally adding coffee beans and a new toaster to the shopping list.

Waiting for the grounds to settle before pushing the plunger, she sniffed the delicious aroma and thought how a smile couldn't stop the world from turning.

Something had, she reminded herself.

She pushed the plunger down slowly, forcing the grounds to the bottom of the jug, then poured two cups, one for Tom, one for herself, hesitating at the kitchen bench, surely not afraid to turn around?

Surely not worried he'd smile again?

'Was it my fault?'

Lauren had, very carefully—wary of smiles—put Tom's cup of coffee on the table in front of him when, right out of the blue, Bobby asked the question.

Startled, she turned to look at the little boy. The usual scowl was gone from his face, but he was frowning, clearly worrying about something.

'The toaster?' she asked, then before he could reply, she added, 'Don't worry, we'll get a new one when we do our grocery shop.'

Bobby shot her a look that clearly said, Stupid woman.

'Greg hitting Mum—was it my fault?' he demanded, his voice cracking slightly so Lauren understood this had been bubbling away inside him for some time.

She knelt beside him but Tom was quicker, lifting Bobby onto his lap and giving him a tight hug before tilting the boy's face up to his.

'Now, you listen to me, young man,' Tom said, gently but firmly. 'There is no way any of what happened between your mum and Greg was anything to do with you.'

Bobby buried his head in Tom's shirt so his next words were muffled, but no less devastating for not being clear.

'He'd say I was a brat and swear about me when he was yelling at her or hitting her so it had to be my fault.'

She saw Tom's arms tighten around the distraught child, and heard him murmuring soothing words, assuring and reassuring Bobby that grown-up people might behave very badly from time to time but it was never the fault of the child or children in their lives.

Echoes in his words resonated deep inside Lauren and she felt she, too, was getting absolution for the guilt and shame she'd carried for so long.

Something worked for Bobby, too. After rubbing his head against Tom's shirt one last time, probably wiping his nose on it, the little boy clambered off Tom's knee, announcing he had to check the washing, and disappeared into the laundry.

Lauren shook her head, her own problems forgotten as she considered what Bobby had been carting around in his young conscience.

'You wouldn't believe we have a child health worker talking all the time to these kids about them not being responsible for adult behaviour. That's the one essential employee at the refuge because we're aware of the damage DV does to the kids who are exposed to it, but we mustn't be using the right approach that Bobby was still worried he was to blame. Are we doing it wrong, Tom?'

He reached out and took her hand, and once again it seemed as if the world had disappeared, leaving only the two of them on the planet, but now wasn't the time for be worrying about whatever was happening in her head—or heart maybe?—she had to work out how to do things better for the children at the refuge.

'I doubt any amount of counselling, or play-acting, or support can take away a child's memories of violence. My parents didn't hit each other but they yelled and no amount of psychology study or analysis or counselling—and, yes, I've had it—has eradicated from my head the sound of their voices screaming abuse at each other as the car crashed and killed them.'

He paused, and Lauren, so shocked to hear what had happened to her friend, turned her hand over so she could squeeze his fingers in silent support.

'You'd think I'd hear the crash, the noise of shrieking metal, maybe even my sister crying out before she died, but, no, I hear their voices...'

'Your sister died as well?'

The words were out before she could stop them, although now they *were* out she had a vague memory of him mentioning the sister being killed.

Tom didn't pause to answer. He was already on his feet, dropping a light kiss on the top of her head, telling her he had to get back to work, and that Alyssa was sleeping but if Lauren could call in later...

He'd had a sister?

Of course there was no reason why she should have known.

Sure, they were friends, but friends didn't tell each other everything.

His sister had also died.

The little boy he'd once been—the one in the strange bed—had lost his whole family?

Water sloshing around her feet brought her back to the present.

'Bobby?'

'It's not my fault!'

And it wasn't. Something had clogged the drain in the tub beside the washing machine—the tub into which the waste-water from the machine ran. By the time they'd cleaned up the mess and hung out the washing—she'd opted not to use the dryer, fearful of what else might go wrong—there was only an hour before the shops shut and they had to put off the visit to the house to get their groceries.

And some time this afternoon or evening she had to visit Alyssa!

Mopping up after Bobby seemed a far easier task...

CHAPTER EIGHT

TOM returned to an empty house but a suspiciously clean kitchen and laundry floor. Having experienced similar problems with his washing machine, he didn't need to see the clothes hanging on the line to understand what had happened.

Small-boy clothes! Surely the sight of a child's clothes hanging on a clothesline couldn't give him a swirling feeling in his stomach. Hunger, that's what it would be. One peanut-butter sandwich did not a lunch make! Although hadn't he had the same feeling when they'd looked at the owls?

Owls—kisses—Lauren…

To distract himself from thoughts he couldn't handle, he looked out at the clothesline again, then frowned. Not all the clothes were new! What looked like the contents of Bobby's entire wardrobe were strung up on the lines. Had some of the clothes been in Joan's case—the case he'd tucked up on a high cupboard—also dirty? He should check.

Or get Lauren to check.

But thinking of Lauren and what she'd been through in her sensitive adolescent years made his stomach swirl again so he turned back to the pantry and refrigerator and made himself another peanut-butter sandwich, just in case it was hunger.

But the peanut-butter sandwich did nothing to chase away the images of Alyssa's battered body, and now his mind kept imposing Lauren's face on the images.

He had to *do* something! Something practical. Joan Sims's suitcases!

He opened the first one, and stared at the contents, completely bewildered by what looked like an open-weave canvas and lots of bits of wool—little bits of wool. Nothing else as far as he could see so he closed the case again, feeling slightly embarrassed to have opened it.

But he desperately needed a diversion and if clothes needed washing…

He opened the second case—normal stuff—toiletries and, yes, clothes, some clean, but a big plastic bag full of garments obviously intended for the laundry.

Tom took the bag through to the laundry, dumped the lot in the machine and got it going, checking first that the outlet wasn't clogged. He considered putting in some of his own clothes—Joan's didn't nearly fill the machine—and put his hand into his pocket, thinking the trousers he had on could go in.

At first he couldn't work out what the piece of paper was, or why he had it, but one glance at the charred edges and he knew. It was whatever Bobby had been burning in the toaster, a picture of something.

This morning seemed a very long time ago, but at least this was another diversion.

Forgetting about adding more clothes to the wash, Tom started the wash then carried the scrap of singed paper into the kitchen and put it down on the table, smoothing the edges carefully so the charred bits didn't break away. He turned it around, studying it from different angles, finally seeing in the darkened paper what looked like the image of a witch—someone with a tall hat anyway.

A magician?

Merlin?

The name floated up from some distant well in his brain. Had he had a book with Merlin the Magician in it?

A favourite book?

Another memory rose from the sludge—Jane reading to him, reading loudly so her voice almost drowned out their parents' shouting.

Someone else was shouting. His visitors! Bobby's voice shrill with what Tom guessed might become a familiar plaint, 'It wasn't my fault.'

Lauren's voice was more controlled. 'Tom, if you're home, could you give us a hand?'

He headed for the front door, pleased to be dragged away from what were becoming very disturbing memories, while the question of why Bobby would be burning a picture of Merlin—or any wizard or witch—still hovered in his mind.

'We shopped,' Lauren explained as he relieved her of a couple of green reusable shopping bags so she could attend to whatever disaster seemed to have befallen Bobby.

'I can see that,' Tom told her, smiling because for all the anguish and emotion of the morning there was something very special in seeing Lauren walking into his house with shopping bags—and *that* thought he'd set aside for further consideration later.

'Bobby's bag had the eggs,' Lauren added quietly, kneeling on the ground beside the boy, who was trying to separate a bottle of tomato sauce from runny, gooey, well-smashed eggs.

'Let's take the whole bag over to the tap and wash things there,' she suggested, and although Bobby's face turned mutinous he did pick up the bag and head towards the outside tap. Lauren detached the hose, but wasn't fast enough to move back as Bobby turned the tap on—hard—so water sprayed all over her and the shopping bag and a large part of the veranda.

To Tom's surprise Lauren didn't protest, simply waiting until Bobby had readjusted the pressure then thanking him for doing it, as if being soaked to the skin was an everyday occurrence. A very damp Lauren pulled the contents of the bag out one by one, and together the pair washed egg off everything, including the bag itself.

'There are more bags in the car if you can drag yourself away from your role as onlooker and carry them in,' Lauren said, and Tom realised he'd stopped at the top of the steps and was still holding the bags he'd taken from her, riveted by the sight of the body the wet clothes revealed.

'I should go over to the hospital,' Lauren said when, clad in clean, dry clothes, she joined him in the kitchen where he was unpacking groceries, supervising Bobby's bringing in of the laundry through the window.

'And I should go with you, at least to introduce you,' Tom told her, thinking more of being there to support Lauren through what would have to be an ordeal than the need for a formal introduction. 'Is Jo still available for babysitting duties?'

Lauren studied the man who'd asked the question. Had there been something more in his voice than the casual words suggested?

'Are you worried I'll fall apart again?' she asked—well, all but demanded as the mess of emotion inside her came back to churning life.

'I'm her doctor,' Tom said gently, and Lauren cringed with shame at her reaction.

Obviously?

She didn't know, but for some reason Tom was holding her again, tucking her body against his chest, brushing his lips in her hair as he murmured assurances at her.

'I would never doubt your professionalism, you must know that,' he was saying, but although the words were calming the churning going on inside her, the warmth of his body against hers was doing other things to other parts of her, sending shivers of excitement along her nerves, down passageways to the apex of her belly, starting up a longing she barely understood in a body that had never felt satisfaction.

This was ridiculous!

Impossible!

What had happened to the professionalism Tom had just assured her she had?

A patient needed her.

That was urgent.

Less urgent but of equal importance was the problem with the refuge.

So why was she wasting precious time clinging to Tom Fletcher like misplaced barnacle?

'Bleagh!'

Bobby had returned and Lauren sprang away from Tom, then, with cheeks she knew must be aflame, she mumbled and bumbled her way back to the conversation.

'Jo—Idon't—perhapsworking—notgood—could you—?'

'That was just a hug, Bobby,' she heard Tom say through the fog in her brain, 'but now I'm going to give Lauren a good kiss so if you don't want to watch and maybe get some pointers, you can turn your back.'

And with that Tom kissed her firmly on the lips, not solving anything because she ended up more confused than ever, the kiss having electrified the shivers into arcs of lightning.

She did manage, eventually, to push away, and find enough words to make a proper sentence.

Several proper, albeit short sentences!

'Jo's working this afternoon. I can introduce myself to Alyssa. Maybe you and Bobby can fix dinner.'

And on that note she fled, although Bobby's strident protest about women's work followed her out the door—heaven only knew what Tom's protest might have been…

* * *

Lauren headed through the hospital, checking with a nurse on the way where she might find Alyssa.

The woman lay very still in the bed, curled into a ball but facing towards the door. Facing potential danger? Her dark hair spread across the pillow, knotted and tangled in places where no doubt she'd twisted and turned, and the brown eyes that opened at Lauren's entrance were dark pools of misery.

'I'm Lauren Cooper, and I'm not here for any particular reason except to see if there's anything I can do for you. Brush your hair? I'm a dab hand with waterless shampoo. I could get you sorted in no time.'

She edged closer as she spoke and was relieved to see a slight smile lighten the woman's beautiful if haggard face.

'I'm a friend of Tom's, the doctor, and I'm also the hospital psychologist if you want to talk to a professional at any time, but for now I thought you might just like someone to talk to as a friend, or just be here with you for a while.'

Alyssa nodded to the chair set against the wall of the small room.

Lauren pulled it closer to the bed, and sat down in it.

'Do you need a hug?' she asked gently, and Alyssa's tiny smile grew a little broader.

'I'm too sore for hugs—bad shoulder,' she whispered, 'but a hand squeeze perhaps?'

Lauren swallowed hard and took the woman's hand, gently squeezing the fingers then clasping the hand in both of hers, sitting quietly while Alyssa became used to her presence in the room.

Eventually Lauren spoke—quietly and carefully.

'I know you wouldn't want your children to see you like this, but would you like me to bring in some photos of them? I know Karen Williams. I could drive over to her place and get some snaps or take some new ones of the kids and print them out on my computer if you'd like recent ones.'

Alyssa's dark eyes studied her in silence then, in a trembling whisper, she asked, 'Not right now but later, would you go and see them? Make sure they're okay. Karen keeps phoning to tell me they are but I need someone to see them.'

The desperation in that husky voice meant Lauren had to swallow again before she could reply.

'I can only imagine how you must feel,' she murmured. 'Of course I'll go but even before I see them I can assure you that if Karen Williams says they're okay, they will be. She's one tough woman!'

There was a brief silence then Alyssa spoke again.

'I suspect she might have had to be,' she whispered.

'What makes you think that?' Lauren asked, although she already suspected the answer. Domestic abuse wasn't genetic, but sons often learnt from their fathers.

'Why else would she be so supportive? Why else would she be backing me against her own son?' Alyssa whispered, tears trickling down her cheeks.

'At least you have her in your corner, and me, and all the hospital staff. You do know that, don't you? No matter who the perpetrator is, domestic violence isn't tolerated in this town. That's one reason we encourage women to report it.'

Alyssa shook her head, not violently but tiredly.

'I just couldn't do it—couldn't go through the court process. I thought I could once before but pulled out and so I know I won't this time. At least, not yet.'

She moved on the bed, shifting with discomfort, then her dark eyes fixed on Lauren's face.

'I remember you from the tree raising. Before the accident. You knew him, didn't you?'

Lauren nodded, understanding exactly what Alyssa had meant by 'knew'.

'Did he hurt you?'

Lauren nodded again, and Alyssa turned her hand so now she was holding Lauren's, two women united in pain, one present, one past…

'It's finished,' Alyssa finally said. 'I kept trying for the girls' sakes. He's a good father, he really is, but not any more. Karen's phoned my father and he'll be here in a day or two. He'll take us home—back to Wisconsin, where we belong.'

Her voice broke on the last words, and she cried again, heartbroken sobs, streaming hot tears, and Lauren understood that they were tears of grief—grief for lost dreams and for the love that couldn't be…

When the storm of emotions ended, Alyssa slipped into a deep and hopefully more restful sleep. Remembering her promise to get photos,

Lauren phoned Tom to check Bobby hadn't burnt down the house, then drove out to the Williams place, about twenty acres nestled in the foothills of the mountains, a sparkling creek running through it, small cabins dotted here and there among the trees.

Dogs barked as she pulled up to open the gate into the house yard of the property and ahead of her she could see two little girls chasing chickens around a shady tree. A photo like that should reassure their mother!

Karen was waiting on the veranda at the top of the steps when Lauren pulled up on the drive. The little girls had scuttled back to the house and now peeped out from behind their grandmother's skirts.

'Lauren Cooper!' Karen said as Lauren emerged from the car. 'You don't know how often I've been thinking about you. About that refuge you run and how I might help, but I guess you've come about Alyssa, not to chat.'

The opening conversation was surprising—even startling—but the light was fading fast and if Lauren wanted outside photos she'd better get going. She dug her camera out of the car.

'I popped in to see Alyssa at the hospital,' she

said as she climbed the steps towards the reception party at the top. 'I thought some pictures of the kids might cheer her up so I wondered if you'd mind if I took some. I can print them off at the office and take them in to her.'

Lauren smiled at the two little girls.

'I'm Lauren,' she said.

The elder girl just stared at her, but the younger, about three, Lauren guessed, was more friendly.

'I'm Eve and that's my sister Zoe,' she said, and gravely put out her hand to shake Lauren's.

Zoe then yielded and put out her hand too, and Lauren shook them both.

'Go and see if you can get the hens back into the pen,' Mrs Williams told the girls, shooing them away with her hands.

It must have been a task the girls were delighted to do, for they went whooping and cheering on their way, leaving Karen and Lauren on the veranda.

'They won't come to any harm out there—the dogs will watch over them. I want to talk to you for a moment.'

Lauren heard the strain in Karen's voice and saw the woman's face was full of pain.

'I'm so ashamed of what he did—a son of mine—but you need to know, everyone needs to know, I'm on Alyssa's side in this and I've got her father coming over to take her home so she'll be safe. But there's something else—the something I should have done earlier. Nat's father was the same and I didn't tell and now I know I should have.'

She paused, looking directly at Lauren.

'I've been thinking of the past and the future for the last three years, since you started the refuge. I want to help there—volunteer—to talk to the women about getting out from under men like that and taking control of their lives. I did it in the end—too late now I know Nat's followed in his father's footsteps—but I made something of myself and I want those women to know they can as well.'

Lauren moved towards her automatically, and took the older woman in a tight, warm hug.

'That would be wonderful,' she said. 'Just wonderful! Everyone in town knows how well you've done with your farm-stay business so it would certainly give the women hope.'

'I'd like to give them more than hope,' Karen continued. 'I'm giving up the farm stay as a business for myself and I want to offer this place to the organisation. The women could use it for weekends and holidays, or they could run it themselves as a farm-stay place. I'd like any women in the house right now to come for Christmas if they'd like that. If Alyssa's still here, it would be good for her too. There are heaps of animals for the kids to play with and plenty for the women to do. What do you think?'

Lauren's mind had, at first, had trouble keeping up, but now it leapt ahead as she envisaged what having a business like this would mean to the refuge. She could keep the safe house open, and find employment for at least some of her charges. There was heaps to work out of course, but...

She gave Karen another huge hug, muttered a thank you, promised to talk soon, then dashed back down the stairs to take photos before the light faded.

'Look!' she said to Alyssa a little later. 'Kids with hens, kids with eggs, kids with the calf, Zoe hugging the big dog, Eve trying to pick up the little dog. They are lovely girls, a real credit to you, and I can assure you they're as happy as they can possibly be with no Mom around right now.'

Alyssa took the photos and leafed through them, smiling and crying at the same time. Finally she propped them up everywhere she could, on the little table, on the stand beside the bed, even handing some back to Lauren and pointing to the window, so Lauren could stick them in the frame.

'Thank you,' she whispered, and held out her hand. Lauren took it and squeezed it again—a hand hug.

'Hair now?' she suggested, and to her surprise Alyssa nodded, so Lauren hurried off to get the things she kept in the bottom of her filing cabinet in the office. She was walking down the passage with her basket of special treats when she ran into Tom.

'Have you persuaded Mike to put Bobby in the lock-up?' she demanded.

Tom grinned at her.

'Close! Very close! Mike did call by just as we'd put the roast in the oven and as he was going over to the refuge and Bobby wanted to look for something over there—some mysterious something that wasn't packed in his luggage—he offered to take him and return him in...'

Tom glanced at his watch.

'Another three-quarters of an hour.'

He peered at the basket she held in her hands. 'Red Riding Hood on her way to Grandma's house?'

Lauren grinned at him and lifted the pink towel that hid the basket's contents.

'Dry shampoo, clean brushes and combs, body moisturiser, hand cream, foot rubs—very refreshing with a touch of mint—revitalising face masks for the serious long-stay patient, in fact, everything that might be needed to pamper someone who's not feeling crash hot.'

He looked up from the basket, right into her eyes, and something in his sent a shiver down her spine, but all he said was, 'You are a good woman, Lauren Cooper.'

He continued on his way, Lauren on hers, although she was distracted from the task in hand as she spread a towel on Alyssa's pillow then sprayed the dry shampoo onto the woman's long dark hair. She chatted away to Alyssa as she brushed and combed, then, finally satisfied, began to massage lotion into Alyssa's hands, but while she was explaining that she'd discovered how much better it made hospitalised women feel if they were pampered a little, her mind was on Tom, and the look she'd seen in his beautiful grey eyes...

Not that a relationship between them could go anywhere, she reminded herself. Relationships meant sex.

At least Tom wouldn't think she was nothing more than a tease.

At least Tom would understand...

The squelch of disappointment in her stomach told her she didn't want Tom understanding. If anything, she wanted him as a lover, but could she handle the physical side of being a lover herself?

Too many question marks hovering in her head. She'd think about the refuge and how they could make, with Karen's help, a home-stay business work. Or think about Bobby.

But thinking about Bobby brought a new squelchy feeling in her stomach. If ever a little boy needed love and stability in his life, it was Bobby.

Could she give him that?

She was sure she could.

But didn't he also need a father?

'Was that good psychology or instinct this afternoon, that you didn't yell at him but let him sort out the tap pressure himself?' the man who wasn't Bobby's father asked Lauren later. They were sitting on the veranda, the roast dinner finished, although a full moon together with streetlights had meant Bobby could still show off his bike skills.

Clad in his new jeans, boots, shirt and cowboy hat, he was doing wheelies on his bike on the front drive, while they acted as audience.

Lauren looked at the man who'd asked the question, a man she knew but, she was realising, didn't really know.

She wondered if he really wanted to know, or if it was her way of avoiding talk of Alyssa and how she, Lauren, had handled the visit.

'I think he's been yelled at enough in his life, or heard enough yelling, and although there are times when I could scream at him, I really, really don't want to do it. Do you know what he was doing when he broke the eggs?'

Tom smiled, and something shifted in her chest, but she couldn't fall in love with Tom—that was a given—so stuff happening in her chest had to be ignored. And who said anything about love?

'Tell me,' the man she wasn't going to love asked quietly, and now it was Lauren's turn to smile.

'He was showing me how you could swing a bucket or a bag around in big circles in the air and stuff didn't fall out of it.'

'Ah, I've done that trick with a bucket of water,' Tom replied, smiling even more broadly so the something in Lauren's chest got worse. 'I got very wet if I remember.'

Picturing the scene, Lauren had to chuckle.

'Well, Bobby was obviously much better at it than you, because nothing fell out but the dozen eggs got jostled by the cans of baked beans and sweet corn and the bottle of tomato sauce, hence the mess.'

'We can buy more eggs,' Tom said, and the 'we' in the sentence told Lauren that she should move out as soon as possible—before this 'we' business went any further—before she started to think that maybe, somewhere along the track, they might actually make a 'we'.

Which she knew full well they wouldn't.

Couldn't.

'Did you see that?'

Bobby's cry brought her attention back to the reason she was here with Tom, living in his house, and feeling all kinds of emotional turmoil because of it.

Bobby was twirling around on the bike, the front wheel off the ground.

'Fantastic!' Tom said, just as Lauren was about to tell the child to stop doing something so dangerous.

'Fantastic?' she echoed, but quietly, as Bobby rode off to try another trick.

'He's trying things, pushing limits,' Tom told her. 'That *is* fantastic! It also shows he's feeling okay—kind of settled with us for all that's happened to him over the weekend.'

Trying things—pushing limits—wasn't that what she had done? Oh, she'd been older than Bobby was—a teenager—but going out with Nat when he'd been known to be wild had maybe pushed the limits too far.

Was that why she'd never told anyone about the abuse?

'I can understand kids wondering if it's their fault their parents are making a mess of life.'

The words came out of her thoughts—unconsidered—and the smile Tom turned on her this time made her wonder if he'd guessed that.

'You should be over feeling shame or blame,' he reminded her, picking up on her thoughts—taking her hand to hold it in his.

'Look at this one!'

Bobby's call distracted them both and they watched him run the bike up a ramp he'd constructed from a brick and a bit of ply he'd found somewhere, then flip it in the air before landing on two wheels, wobbling slightly but carrying on, one arm raised in triumph as he yelled his success to the heavens.

They clapped and shouted praise, but as he spun away, Tom squeezed Lauren's hand and they sat and watched the boy until the wind blowing in from the ocean turned cold and Lauren called him Bobby to bed.

But when the bathed, pyjama-clad child came into the kitchen to say goodnight, Tom remembered the scrap of paper Lauren had rescued from the toaster.

He pulled it out of his pocket and laid it on the table.

'Why did you want to burn it, Bobby?' he asked gently, then felt like a monster when tears welled in Bobby's eyes.

''S nothing!' Bobby growled, pushing away from the table. He slammed his chair back with such force it toppled over, and once on his feet he snatched at the singed and blackened scrap, clutching it to his chest as he dashed from the room, heading for his bedroom.

'At least he didn't run away,' Lauren said quietly.

'Unless he's in there packing,' Tom muttered, wondering why on earth he'd spoiled a pleasant evening by bringing up something Bobby obviously wanted forgotten.

'What was on it?' Lauren asked.

Tom saw the anxiety in her voice mirrored in her eyes, and *had* to touch her again, reaching across the table to rest his hand on hers.

'I don't know—it was too badly burned to tell, although it *seemed* to be a picture of a witch or a wizard perhaps, but I couldn't really tell.'

'Merlin!' Lauren breathed, her face lightening with the word as though the magic of the legendary man was working within her. 'Of course! I wonder where it is?'

'Where Merlin is?' Tom looked around. 'Wasn't he a shape-shifter? Could he be my oven, or perhaps my washing machine? It's definitely possessed!

Lauren laughed and Tom found the rage he'd been holding at bay was gone, replaced, yet again, by the strange contentment he kept finding in the simple presence of this woman in his house.

'It's a rug Joan was making for Bobby. He loves all things Merlin. I imagine he saw a movie at some time that had Merlin in it and now he knows things I didn't know. For instance, in my mind Merlin was always connected with King Arthur, but Bobby informed me he was around long before that.'

She grinned at Tom across the table before adding, 'I must admit I was so suspicious that he'd know such a thing that I looked it up and he was right. If there was a real Merlin—or a person Merlin might have been based on—then he was around way before the legends of King Arthur began.'

Unfortunately—or perhaps fortunately for Tom's peace of mind—the smile gave way to a frown as Lauren continued, 'Maybe it's at the refuge. That's what he went to look for earlier with Mike.'

Tom met her frown with one of his own. He was totally bamboozled now.

'What's at the refuge?' he demanded.

'The rug, of course. I'll go over there later but right now I'd better reassure Bobby.'

She left the room while Tom's mind replayed the conversation, finally settling on 'a rug Joan was making' as the most salient part of it. Canvas and bits of wool? A rug in progress?

He didn't want to get Bobby's hopes up by mentioning it right now, but as soon as he was through the goodnight session with the little boy, now soothed by reassurances from Lauren, he'd check that suitcase again.

In the bedroom Lauren was reading the bedtime story, and standing in the doorway, looking at the fondness—no, love—in her face as she looked down at Bobby, he felt a surge of—it had to be protectiveness—so strong he had to lean against the doorjamb for a moment.

It was the family thing again.

CHAPTER NINE

'I⊤ *is* the rug,' Lauren said a little later, lifting the mess of canvas and wool out of the suitcase and spreading it on the table. 'And, see, it's nearly finished.'

She looked up at Tom, eyes gleaming with excitement.

'I know there are two rug hooks because sometimes one of the helpers worked with Joan. There's not so much to do—let's get it done tonight.'

She was practically shimmering with expectation—and no way could he pour water on *that* shimmer!

But…

'Hook a rug? You're talking to a man who has to get the dry cleaners to sew his buttons on!'

'It's easy. I'll show you!' Lauren declared, which was how Dr Tom Fletcher, who normally on a Monday night might be enjoying a little female company, found himself sitting at his kitchen table, pushing bits of wool through holes and knotting them to make sure they stayed in place.

Which was fine as far as it went, but working on a small rug—Merlin the magician or not—meant sitting in very close proximity to Lauren, feeling her warmth, her softness when she moved, breathing in the clean, fresh scent of her, blowing fine fair hair out of his face when she spun to fix something for him.

He hooked and tied and hooked and tied and all the while the urge to take this woman in his arms grew stronger and stronger.

'Concentrate!' Lauren chided at one stage, but her voice seemed a little shaky, the rebuke far from firm.

Was she feeling it as well?

Could something as simple as hooking a rug have brought another dimension into their relationship?

His body certainly seemed to think so! Yes, they touched from time to time, skin meeting skin, thigh meeting thigh, hard to avoid it, but even when they weren't touching he could feel her presence, feel it tantalising his body in a way he couldn't remember feeling before.

Was it because she was off limits? Not only because she'd already rejected him or because of what had happened in the past, but because she was a guest in his house—definitely off limits! So could the heat building in his body be put down to the lure of forbidden fruit?

He hoped so.

He really did!

'Okay, we're done!' she declared, some hours later.

'Just as well, given it's after midnight,' Tom grouched, although his chest filled with pride and he all but forgot the heat as Lauren lifted the finished product, holding up the picture of the bearded old man in his tall, pointed hat.

'It's fantastic!' he said, and he leapt to his feet, knocking over his chair as Bobby had earlier. But who cared about the chair? He grabbed Lauren and the rug in a tight clasp and swung her around in the air. 'We did it!' he crowed. 'We did it!'

After which it was only natural that he should kiss her, and although there was two inches of tightly knotted wool between her body and his,

his heart surged with a wild emotion when her lips fluttered uncertainly for a moment before opening beneath his kiss and, suddenly, there was Lauren kissing him back…

They had two inches of wool and carpet between their bodies so it couldn't be the siren song of lust that had her returning Tom's kiss. But returning it she was, drawn into it by some emotion too powerful to resist.

It was just a kiss—a celebratory kiss—nothing more, she kept telling herself, yet her lips clung to his, opening to his invading tongue, revelling in the moist warmth, the sharing, the sheer physical delight that kissing Tom was spreading through her body.

She tingled in places she hadn't known existed, heated in places she knew shouldn't be so hot, her nerve endings quivered and her hands began to tremble so she let go of the rug, which remained firmly stuck between them, and clasped her hands around Tom's neck, sliding her fingers into his hair—silky hair that stirred her quivering nerves even more.

Maybe it was because the whole time they'd been

working on the rug, sitting so close to each other, her body had been feeling things it shouldn't, alive with an excitement she didn't understand—well, she did understand it, she just didn't want to think about why she'd been feeling it!

The kiss deepened and she clung to him more tightly, all questions forgotten.

Tom had shifted too. His arms had been clasped around her, but now *his* hands were in *her* hair, and it seemed, although she was probably imagining it, that his fingers were trembling too...

He whispered her name, the all-but-soundless 'Lauren' seeming to float from his lips, wrapping her in a bubble of new sensation.

A tiny mew of protest fell from hers when his mouth lifted for that fraction of a second, and though it was a wordless noise he seemed to understand for the kiss resumed and she allowed herself to stop thinking altogether, to stop analysing and categorising her sensory reactions and just enjoy them as tendrils of physical delight bound them together.

Could a kiss last for ever?

So it seemed to Lauren, although eventually they drew apart, as if by some mutual but unspoken agreement, the rug falling to the floor between them, Merlin the magician a crumpled bundle on the floor.

It was a moment in time, Lauren realised, when they—or maybe she—could move forward, and though she was confused about where such a choice might lead—confused about the whole situation—she knew the decision was up to her.

Excitement urged her forward, while fear held her back—no, not fear, for she knew Tom would never hurt her, but trepidation…

'I think I have to trim the top of it,' Lauren whispered, bending to pick it up, knowing there was fierce colour in her face and hoping Tom might assume it was because she'd bent over.

He looked at her, saying nothing, studying her as if she were a new acquaintance, or perhaps a chance-met old one, until, when the silence had stretched, it seemed, for even longer than the kiss, and the rug was grasped in front of her in a white-knuckled grip, he asked, 'That's it?'

She tried for calm, control and composure.

'What's it?' she asked, and he turned and walked away, along the hall, down the steps, heading who knew where.

Lauren sat down at the table, picked up Joan's sharp scissors, and began to trim the uneven ends of wool until the rug was smooth and thick and a perfect representation of the wizard Bobby so admired.

Tom checked his patients in the hospital, looking in on Alyssa who was sleeping, a nurse never far away, keeping watch over the fragile and vulnerable woman. He couldn't help but picture Lauren lying there and the cold anger filled him again, although this time the heat that lingered in his body from the kiss had diluted it, allowing him to consider the things he'd learned.

Lauren's disjointed confession of her abuse bothered him in many ways. Was she still suffering the after-effects? *Was* that why she hadn't dated since he'd known her?

He wasn't vain enough to think it was why she hadn't dated him, but if she *was* still avoiding intimacy…

As if he could help her! he scoffed to himself.

Oh, he knew physical intimacy extremely well, but helping someone over any other kind of problem with intimacy—well, hardly! Not when he'd avoided it all his life!

Yet deep inside he felt a need to do something for the woman who was living in his house—for the friend he'd found in Lauren.

For the woman he'd kissed?

Well…

The only thing he did know was that it wasn't his old friend Lauren whom he'd kissed, or she who'd kissed him back. Something had shifted in their relationship, and as they were bound together by their responsibility to a lost and lonely little boy, he'd darned well better get it shifted back.

He returned to the house, making a noise as he came up the steps, hoping she'd hear him and come out so they could talk.

At two in the morning?

She didn't, but when he found his duvet back on his bed, he looked into Bobby's room, seeing, on the floor beside the bed, the finished rug—carefully placed there as a surprise for Bobby when he woke up.

That was so typical of Lauren—the Lauren who sought to make people's lives easier and happier, their paths smoother—that he smiled and for a moment forgot the Lauren that he'd kissed...

Had there been a promise implicit in that kiss?

This was the question running through Lauren's head as she tossed and turned on the very comfortable bed in the second spare bedroom of Tom's house.

On her part, not his, she meant.

Tiredness made her thoughts swirl uselessly around in her head, while her body continued to whisper traitorous messages.

But Tom deserved better than to be led on by promises, then rejected when she turned frigid at the first really intimate touch.

On top of which would be her humiliation when that happened—the numbing despair and overwhelming embarrassment.

In front of Tom?

She couldn't contemplate such a thing so, no, there had been no promise implicit in the kiss, and if, by chance he'd read one, she'd surely made things clear when she'd grabbed the rug as if it were a lifeline, chattering on about trimming it.

She must have slept, although as she leapt out

of bed in response to Bobby's yell, she knew it hadn't been for nearly long enough. Near numb with fatigue, she rushed to Bobby's room, to find him dancing up and down on the little rug.

'Look, it's here!' he cried. 'It's finished. My Merlin rug. Mum made it—she must have finished it without telling me. Look!'

He grabbed it off the floor and held it up for inspection, and Tom, who'd joined Lauren in the entrance to the room, put his arm around her waist and gave her a gentle squeeze, sharing the pleasure of their achievement and the joy of the little boy.

'It was in a suitcase at the house,' Tom told Bobby, while Lauren pleased the boy by examining the rug more closely, exclaiming over it while hoping he wouldn't notice a couple of blisters from the rug hook on her hands.

'It's beautiful,' Lauren told Bobby as he took his treasure back and held it crumpled tightly in his arms. Tears shone in his eyes and she drew him close, so once again she was hugging someone with the rug between them.

If she hadn't raised her eyes to Tom it would have been much easier to go with the pretence of no invitation in a kiss, but the flare of complicity in Tom's eyes, and the slight smile on his lips, told her it wouldn't be that easy.

Fortunately, because she was feeling totally lost—way out of her depth in a sea of emotion she didn't understand—Tom took control of the morning routine.

'Breakfast?' he suggested, and Bobby pulled away from Lauren.

'We've got Frosty Flakes!' he told Tom, darting out of the room, the rug dropped to the floor.

'Clothes and bathroom first,' Tom said, as Lauren bent to straighten the rug. 'Wash face and hands, clean teeth, get dressed. We'll all have breakfast together.'

To Lauren's surprise, Bobby trotted obediently towards the bathroom, then she looked down at the Cupids on her nightgown and wished she'd beaten him to it.

But she *could* get changed.

'Lauren!'

Too late! Tom's had rested his hand on her shoulder, catching her as she turned away from him, and though her nerves jangled at his touch, and fear he'd bring up the promise in the kiss stiffened all her muscles, he simply smiled and said, 'We did good, huh?'

The slang expression made her smile and she raised her hand to exchange a high five with him, then darted to her room, reminding herself that touching any part of Tom, even the palm of his hand in a high five, was fraught with danger and would only make her decision to deny her reactions to the kiss even harder.

As it turned out, Tom was called to the hospital before the first Frosty Flake was poured then after breakfast Bobby was whipped away by the mother of a friend of his from school, who'd phoned first to ask if he would like to go down to Port Macquarie with her and her son. Her older boy would be with them, she'd explained, and the three lads could go to a movie while she did some last-minute Christmas shopping.

Which left Lauren on her own and with plenty of time to visit Alyssa once again. She went into the office first to check for messages and mail and was about to leave when Tom walked in.

'Did you come over to see Alyssa?' he asked, and something in his voice made her look more closely at him, although looking too closely at Tom was something she'd been avoiding this morning.

His face was drawn, and he paused before adding, 'She was pregnant, Lauren. She's lost the baby. I did a D and C this morning so she'll still be a bit woozy.'

Her mission forgotten—for the moment—Lauren slumped down into her chair.

'Hell and damnation,' she muttered. 'The poor woman!'

Tom shrugged and shook his head, looking not defeated exactly but so down, it took iron control on Lauren's part to prevent herself standing up, crossing to him, and giving him a hug. She knew how much he loved obstetric work and how hard he took such occurrences, and a comforting hug would have been natural.

It's what she would have done before all this began, she reminded herself.

Even yesterday she would have hugged him, before she'd cut the tendrils of desire that had wrapped around the two of them with that stupid rug remark…

He hesitated in the doorway. Was he waiting for the hug?

She *wasn't* going to hug him!

And eventually he walked away, leaving Lauren feeling guilty that she hadn't offered *some* kind of comfort.

Except it would have had to be a hug.

It's what she did.

To her, gathering someone in a strong embrace often did more good than a thousand words. As well as offering comfort, hugs could transfer energy. They could invigorate and rejuvenate, and unlike drugs they had no unpleasant side effects. She knew enough of her own psychology to know she'd taken to hugs as a way of initiating physical contact with people back at a time when it had been very difficult for her to be touched. Back then she'd realised that the hugger could break away any time—the one who hugged was in control and control had been very important to her.

Hugging Tom, however, was a very different matter. Hugging Tom would have side effects for her—not unpleasant but unsettling, tempting—*stupid*!

She'd go and see Alyssa—give her a hand hug and sit with her a while—then go over to the refuge and work out the Christmas plans for the families in the house. Tell them about Karen Williams's offer and see what they thought…

Bobby returned mid-afternoon, full of talk about his day's adventure, the movie—not that good—and the treat they'd had, eating at a fast-food outlet. Lauren had slipped a casserole into the oven, thinking the vegetables in with the cubes of lamb might be well enough disguised for Bobby to eat them without complaint.

'Can we go over to the house and show the kids there my new clothes?' he asked, when he'd finished describing his day.

'I thought you might be tired,' Lauren said, while wondering if his ability to latch onto something and not let go was a normal 'kid' thing, or a 'Bobby' thing. She'd been certain he'd have forgotten about showing off his new clothes by now.

'I suppose we can,' she said, 'but we can only stay an hour or so because dinner's in the oven.'

'What is it?' her new protégé demanded, suspicion flashing in his eyes.

'A casserole.'

'Yuck—sloppy stew! Why can't we have sausages?'

'Because you need a balanced diet, we all do, and there is no way I'm cooking one thing for you and something else for me and Tom. You'll just have to handle the sloppy stew tonight. Tomorrow we might have chicken.'

She expected to see the scowl he brought out when things didn't go his way, but to her surprise he grinned then dashed off, presumably to get dressed in his new clothes.

They stayed longer than they'd intended at the refuge. The women were so excited at the prospect of taking their children to a farm for Christmas they wanted every detail, and Bobby was having a good time with the children he knew so he'd been happy to stay. As a result the sun was sinking towards the horizon when they drove home, and even the usually indefatigable Bobby was showing signs of tiredness.

'There's Tom!' Bobby shouted as they pulled up in the drive. Lauren turned her head and saw the man she was avoiding thinking about walking towards the house. Hard not to think about him when just seeing him made her heart jolt in her chest.

They got out of the car and waited until he joined them, Lauren sniffing the air, sure she'd smell the delicious aroma of a simmering casserole as she walked through the door.

Perhaps the breeze was blowing it the other way.

They all headed for the kitchen, which had fast become the hub of their little household, Bobby yammering away at Tom, Lauren growing more anxious about the casserole.

She crossed to the oven and felt the outside.

Cold!

'Problem?' Tom asked, and she turned to see him smiling, but with that one eyebrow raised.

Big problem, her mind replied as she battled her reaction to that smile, so by the time she was ready to reply he, too, was feeling the oven.

'It helps to turn it on,' he said, standing so close she could feel the warmth of his body, while the smile that accompanied the words exacerbated all the tremors and tingling and heat rioting within her body.

'I *did* turn it on, look!'

Indignation helped and she stepped back to point at the dials, but for some reason a nothing exchange of words about an oven was proving as seductive as that darned kiss had been and she was losing strength in her knees and willpower in her mind.

Could he be feeling it?

She had no idea!

Her experience was limited, and in retrospect mostly embarrassing, so she had no idea if the man peering into the depths of his oven, poking at things with his fingers—he *had* turned it off first—was feeling anything other than aggravation that his oven was broken.

'It worked okay last night when we cooked the lamb,' Tom said, turning a mystified face towards Lauren as she stood there beside him, contrarily revelling in all the sensations his closeness was causing when she should have been moving to Antarctica.

A snigger from somewhere behind them gave the game away, Lauren catching on first and turning on the eight-year-old demon who had come into their lives.

'What did you do?' she demanded.

'Nothin'!'

The predictable response was accompanied by a hurt look but Tom had sussed Bobby out, turning on the switch for the kitchen light and finding it, too, wasn't working.

'Power board,' he said to Lauren. He grasped

Bobby gently by the shoulder and steered him towards the back door. 'Now you'll turn it back on, young man, and any more of those tricks and the bike goes into storage for a week, understand?'

An outwardly contrite Bobby turned the power back on, explaining to Tom as he did so that one of the big kids from school had once turned off the power to all the houses in their street.

'Inwardly the little devil's gloating,' Lauren said to Tom, as Bobby went into the living room to watch a TV show while she found something else to have for dinner. 'He wanted sausages, not sloppy stew for dinner.'

'So we can't let him win, can we?' Tom told her, enfolding her in a smile that made her heart melt. 'What else do we have?'

'Look for yourself. There's cold meat, salad, cheese—things I bought for sandwiches for lunches.'

Tom poked his head into the refrigerator, then started to haul stuff out.

'When I was a kid I hated salads, so maybe a salad will be a just punishment.'

The smile this time was more of a grin but it had the same effect. She had to get out of there and, speaking of that—thinking of it—why hadn't they heard from Mike, or someone from Children's Services?

And why hadn't *she* phoned around to find out what was happening in the search for Bobby's relatives?

Surely not because she was enjoying living here?

'I'll just check he hasn't found the water main,' she said, and fled the kitchen, needing to get away from Tom while she worked out just what was happening in her head.

Was she escaping him? Tom wondered as he watched Lauren whisk from the room.

And if so, why?

Surely she hadn't been feeling the tug of attraction he'd felt as they'd stood at the oven! It was an *oven*, for heaven's sake, and a none-too-clean one at that! Yet he'd lingered there, mind blank for all he'd been poking things, his body revelling in being close to Lauren's, drinking in the hint of the dusky perfume she used, the softness of the hair that brushed his face as she moved.

He had to do something about this—maybe go visit Emily at Belrose, although that would be the act of a cad, using one woman to forget another, and he'd never done caddish things…

He made a salad instead—the old-fashioned kind of salad his foster-mothers had always made. Trendy, tossed in a bowl then dumped on a plate salads were all very well, but for someone like him—and Bobby—who liked individual tastes, a pile of grated cheese next to the mound of grated carrot beside the slices of tinned beetroot and the slices of ham and tomato was how a salad should be. He put the three plates in the refrigerator and went to find his 'family'.

They were on the front veranda, Lauren gently questioning Bobby about relatives.

'I haven't *got* any grandparents,' Bobby protested. 'There used to be an old lady Mum called Aunty but she died. We never saw her anyway 'cos she lived in Sydney.'

Not wanting to interrupt, Tom watched from the doorway, studying Bobby carefully and deciding the child wasn't upset by this lack of relations. If anything, he seemed to accept it as the natural way of things.

'I don't need any old relations,' Bobby continued. 'I can just stay here with you and Tom.'

Tom's attention switched to Lauren. How would she handle this?

'For the moment, definitely,' she said, reaching out and rubbing Bobby's thatch of hair. 'The problem is that there are rules about who children live with, and there are people whose job it is to find the best places for kids to live and it might be they find a nice aunt or uncle you didn't know you had and it might be that aunt or uncle would *like* you to live with them.'

'Would not!'

Bobby's denial was so swift Tom moved, thinking he might strike out again, but he remained sitting in the chair, staring out at the darkening sea, his jaw set in a way Tom now recognised as a fight against tears.

'Who's for some dinner?' he called from the doorway, then he stepped onto the veranda where he, too, ruffled Bobby's hair. 'Cold salad, thanks to you, champ,' he said. 'And don't bother telling me you don't like salad. You're a growing boy, you need your vegetables.'

Bobby rose without a murmur and to Tom's surprise the child put his arms around Tom's waist and gave him a hug. He quite possibly wiped his wet eyes and dribbly nose against Tom's shirt at the same time, but what did that matter, compared to a hug from a lonely, confused, bereaved little boy?

They sat at the table in the kitchen, and as Tom put the plates on the table he couldn't help but feel a sense of…not pride exactly but deep satisfaction, as if somehow he'd made a family.

'I like salads like this.' Bobby's appreciative comment broke into Tom's slightly shocked consideration of how the words 'family' and 'satisfaction' had wormed their way into the same sentence in his mind. He, who was happy as a loner…

'And I'm sorry, Lauren, about the 'lectric switch.'

Lauren smiled at the miscreant.

'Not to worry,' she said easily, then turned the smile a little brighter. 'Just think, you can have the casserole tomorrow.'

Bobby grimaced but didn't object, apparently accepting defeat in the matter of sloppy stews!

'No relations?' Tom asked. It was some hours later. Bobby was asleep in bed, barely lasting out his second bedtime story, his face angelic in the glow of the small night-light Lauren had found for him.

Now his temporary parents were sitting on the veranda, enjoying an after-dinner coffee and the peaceful sound of the waves washing on the beach below the town.

Lauren turned towards him, the light behind her so her face was shadowed, but he could hear real concern in her voice when she answered.

'Would you believe I didn't even try to find any relations today? I saw him off with his friends, then went across to the hospital, got involved with Alyssa and had a talk to Karen Williams, came back and prepared dinner, and didn't at any stage give a thought to Bobby's future.'

She sighed so deeply he wanted to touch her— to comfort her—but touching Lauren was habit-forming, and possibly addictive, and definitely not a good idea given even standing near her had fired his body to an aching desire.

'Not only did I not do anything about the poor kid, but I don't want to think about *why* I didn't contact anyone,' she finished.

'You're not in charge of finding relations,' he reminded her, surprised to find himself in sympathy with her over not wanting to contact people. 'Mike's handling that with Children's Services and it's up to them, not us. All we're doing is looking after him for now, making sure he feels secure, and knows he's safe with us.'

I think, he added to himself...

'Except if we don't find some relation soon, I'll have to talk to him about Joan's funeral. He's a little boy, Tom, he shouldn't have to be involved in things like that, yet what happens if I don't talk about it and later find he wanted input? Maybe there's a song Joan liked that he'd like to hear played. I don't know!'

Forget the aching desire—this was a woman who needed a hug!

Tom stood up, hauled her out of her chair and put his arms around her.

'*We'll* talk to him,' he told her firmly. '*We'll* help him decide what he wants—together! And if he doesn't want to know—or if he doesn't want anything to do with any of it—then we'll back him up on that, but you're right, we do have to talk to him.'

He felt her body relax against his, her curves fitting into him as if they'd been fashioned to match his shape, and the desire he'd been trying to forget burned through him, so his muscles tensed and his arms drew her closer, closer, closer, until he was pressing kisses on the top of her head, on her forehead, on her eyelids, working slowly downwards until she lifted her head to him and pressed a kiss onto his lips.

Lauren kissing *him*?

He needed no second invitation, his mouth opening over hers, devouring her lips, seeking entry to her sweet, moist warmth, coffee flavoured but Lauren flavoured as well. Soft breasts pressed against his chest, moving now and then when she dragged in a deep, replenishing breath before returning all her attention to the kiss.

The Kiss—it was assuming capital letters in his head, for never had kissing someone been so satisfying. Generally seeing it as little more than a prelude to making love, he usually got the kissing part over and done with quite quickly, but right now he didn't want this kiss to stop.

Her arms had crept around his waist, her hands sliding up, then down, cupping his butt, squeezing it, holding him tightly to her, evidence of his arousal pressed into the softness of her belly.

She moved against him, moved enough to make him groan.

Stupid!

Why make a sound?

Now she was gone, slamming away from him so suddenly she nearly fell.

He caught her—saved her from falling—held her steady, watching her chest rise and fall as she sucked in air—saw the tears in her eyes and the quiver on her lips as she tried to speak and failed.

And when finally a word did emerge, it was hardly what he'd expected. It was a trembling and shame-faced 'Sorry', stricken eyes raised to his, panic as well as embarrassment written on her face.

He drew her close again, and held her, just held her.

'Sorry for kissing me?' he asked gently, when her trembling had eased and she'd once again relaxed against him.

Well, almost relaxed against him…

She shook her head, then lifted it—no coward, his friend Lauren.

'Sorry for—for leading you on—for encouraging you—for kissing you like that. Sorry I'm so damn inept at this stuff. Sorry I'm not what you need, Tom. Believe me.'

She paused, as if waiting for him to say something, but what could he say? Besides, silence often
worked because the person who found the silence
most awkward would fill it...

And finally she did!

'You know my history—you've seen Alyssa in
hospital. I know as a psychologist I should have
sorted myself out by now, but...'

Even in the shadowy light of the veranda he
could see the colour in the cheeks and pain for
her—for her embarrassment and for the things
she'd suffered in the past—shafted through Tom's
body.

'I'm no good with intimacy.'

She didn't mumble the words, or try to hide her
face against his chest, although it was there, read-
ily available to her. She looked up into his eyes as
she said it, defying the flaming cheeks and quivering voice that evidenced her embarrassment.

'I have had boyfriends since Nat, Tom. Heaven
knows, it's been a long time, and I've tried. I've
truly tried, but comes the time—well, the important time—and I can't do it. I go rigid. I'm no good
to you for all I'd like to be...'

Tears slid down her scarlet cheeks and Tom

folded his arms around her and wondered how she'd take it she knew he'd like to mingle his tears with hers, as his pain for her took on another dimension—sinking to a depth he hadn't known he could feel.

He held her and he rubbed his hands across her back, offering comfort, nothing more. She snuggled into him, accepting comfort.

When it changed he had no idea, but change it did, with Lauren raising her face again, kissing him, cautiously at first, eyes wary, questioning, yet her body responding to his touch.

He eased himself away, and looked into those changeable eyes.

'Are you doing this for me? Do you feel obliged in any way?'

She flushed, the colour so delicate he had to touch her cheek to feel the warmth.

She shook her head, her gaze roaming his face as if some answer to an unasked question might be loitering there.

She opened her mouth to speak, closed it again, shrugged, then finally said, 'It's probably the opposite. I think *I* might be using *you*.'

It nearly broke his heart.

The heart he hadn't thought he had.

The kind of heart you had to have to experience love...

He wanted to say please use him all she liked, but knew that would be crass. He wanted to say he'd do anything for her, whatever she wanted, but couldn't have explained why. He wanted, more than anything, to make love to her and that thought shocked him so much he couldn't speak at all.

He didn't make love. Making love wasn't in his repertoire, he practised mutually enjoyable sex.

'You'd rather not?' she asked.

He looked at the woman he hadn't answered while all these confusing thoughts had been racing through his head.

'I don't know what I'd rather,' he admitted. 'Going further—and, yes, I'm so attracted to you I'd like nothing more, and forget the using-me part, that's nonsense—but going further could complicate our lives. Do you realise that?'

She studied him again.

'You mean if it didn't work? If we weren't suited? When we part but have to work together? Is that what you're thinking?'

'All of those,' he told her, but he kissed her

anyway. 'But aren't we getting ahead of ourselves here?'

Lauren didn't know.

In point of fact, she knew nothing—absolutely nothing. Her brain had ceased to work while her body ached with a raw need that the kissing had generated, and which now pulsed through her body like a high-voltage charge.

She'd warned Tom what might happen if they went further.

He couldn't say he didn't know.

And he'd warned her of future consequences.

'I don't care,' she whispered to him, and kissed him again, giving in to the sensations his firm but gentle touch was sending into all parts of her body, the brush of his fingers across her breasts spearing more need down between her thighs. She squirmed against him, mindless, barely registering his suggestion they move into the bedroom, barely aware of Tom closing the door behind them, leading her to that great raft of a bed, talking, touching, soothing, exciting, then soothing again, damping down fires before recharging them, her limbs now boneless, her nerves quivering, the charged wanting something she had never felt before.

'Just touch my face at any time you want to stop. Or say the word,' Tom whispered, his voice muffled as he spoke against a wet patch on her neck, a patch he'd licked and kissed and teased until she turned and twisted with desire, not knowing how to do the same to him, to excite him as much as he was exciting her.

Her first touch was so tentative he may not have felt it, but the warmth of his skin sent a tingle through her nerve endings so she splayed her hands across his chest, pushing his shirt to one side, relishing her own responses, learning the hardness of his muscles, the shape of his chest, a light line of hair arrowing downwards.

Follow it?

Did she dare?

Lost in the haze of sensations that were her body's response to Tom's ministrations, she felt her body relax, giving in to the jolt of pleasure his touch on her nipple produced, giving in to the quiver of anticipation as his questing hands slid lower. But she wanted to be more than a passive recipient of these delicious sensations, she wanted to explore, be part of the game, to learn what gave him pleasure while still discovering it herself. She let her fingers slide lower, and lower, Tom's hand now joining hers, helping her cup him, *his* hand moving to brush across her mound, shooting new darts of excitement through her body.

The silky skin firmed beneath her touch, Tom's finger probed gently into her, while excitement skittered now, her breathing slowed…

'Are you okay?'

Tom's husky words drifted through the air around them, but Lauren could barely discern their meaning. She knew she'd passed the bounds of other experiences—knew too that they'd *never* been like this—and most of all she knew she didn't want to stop.

'I'm pretty sure I am,' she managed to reply, but now his fingers were working some magic on her body so it came out as a strangled squeak.

Was it Tom's experience or because it *was* Tom, a man she was fairly sure she loved, that had released her from the memories of the past, the fear of pain that had probably built up in her mind to a level beyond any she had felt?

Her woozy mind lost the thread about then, and her body didn't care about the answer. All it wanted was more of the same. Perhaps some release somewhere along the line, from the tension—exquisite tension—that was building and building in her body...

Then it came, the release, lifting her high into the air, the world in limbo as all thoughts and memories disappeared and she was lost to sheer sensation.

She shattered, pressed against Tom, came apart again, then, knowing she needed more—*he* needed more—she drew him into her body, clasping him inside her, moving again until she heard him gasp and felt his long-withheld release. She held him to her, relishing the weight of him on her body, wondering if his weight would help her put herself together again...

'I never knew!'

She wasn't certain how much later this was, if they'd slept or just lain together, but finally she'd found the words. Not the 'Thank you' she probably should have said, but the words to reveal her wonder—the miracle of it all...

He was gone when she woke in the morning, leaving her alone in the enormous bed, and inevitably all the things they'd considered the previous night about complicating things came rushing back to her. Questions she'd never considered hammered in her head.

How did she face a man when she'd done things like she'd done to him during the long night? How to face him without blushing? How to look at him without thinking of him naked? Without remembering how he'd felt inside her?

Fortunately, the sound of Bobby stirring—yawning loudly was Bobby's way of announcing he was awake—in the next room reminded her of her responsibilities and while a rush of shame—how could they have done *that* with Bobby in the house?—swept through her, she got out of bed, clutched her discarded clothes to her, and bolted to her bedroom, where she hurriedly dressed and raced to the kitchen so she could pretend she'd been there all along when Bobby did appear.

Except Tom was there before her, making coffee, smiling at her. And forget blushing, she was certain her whole body had turned scarlet. Was that how scarlet women got their name? She'd lost her mind, obviously, and was now standing in the kitchen door, staring at Tom, thinking totally irrational thoughts and with no idea how to retrieve a little sanity.

'Coffee?' Tom asked, as if it was just an ordinary morning, although maybe his smile was just a little softer—teasing almost?

'In a cup? With milk and sugar how you like it?' he persisted.

Apparently she hadn't answered him, but how could she when her mind was replaying every instant of last night and her eyes couldn't take in enough of his strong-boned face, a shadow of black stubble on his chin, his lips curled into the very slightest of smiles, and his broad, muscled chest, tanned skin spread like satin over it, the little pathway of hair—

Heat flooded her again but now at least she'd found some words.

'You could at least have pulled on a shirt!' she muttered at him, and he laughed, then set down the coffee pot and came towards her, sliding his arm around her shoulders and giving her a hug, and then a swift kiss.

It was interrupted before it could be anything but swift by Bobby's 'Bleagh!'

Somehow they got through breakfast—Lauren

recovering slightly once Tom *did* pull on a shirt—but although she'd expected him to head off to the hospital as soon as the meal was finished, he lingered, helping with the dishes, hanging around, finally suggesting they all sit on the veranda for a while.

Something in the way he spoke brought Lauren out of her confusion over the night's events and a cold shiver of presentiment rushed through her. Had Mike been in touch—had he found Bobby's family? Or maybe 'things being different' meant Tom had had enough of them staying with him…

Lauren made more coffee—she'd need something to keep her going!—and joined Tom and Bobby on the veranda.

'We need to talk, Bobby,' Tom began. 'I know you're only a kid, but because it's about your mother we do need to talk to you about what happens next.'

'I ain't got no relations!' Bobby said, and stood up, ready to flee if there was any suggestion of him going to someone he didn't know.

'It's not about relations, it's about business,' Tom said, and with a wave of relief she shouldn't have felt, Lauren caught on. She reached out and took Bobby's hand, pulling him onto her knee.

'Remember,' she said gently, 'when Carrots the red guinea pig at the refuge died—what did we do?'

Bobby squirmed on her knee then turned and faced her.

'We buried it. We had a—whatya call it—funeral.'

'We did,' Lauren said. 'And we sang some songs and some of the kids talked and then we had a little party because Carrots had been a really good guinea pig and we were saying thank you to him for making us happy.'

'So?'

Tom watched Lauren's face. In fact, though he hoped he wasn't being obvious, he'd been watching Lauren's face since he'd woken up—at first watching her sleep beside him, her serene beauty catching at his heart, and then when she'd come into the kitchen, doubt and wonder mingling in her eyes, embarrassment colouring her cheeks. He'd read no regret, which had relieved him enormously, and now he was just watching—waiting—wondering just how she was going to get from the guinea pig to Joan…

When he'd started the conversation he hadn't known how he'd get there either, so had been relieved when Lauren had caught on, but now?

'With people, Bobby,' Lauren was saying quietly, holding Bobby against her in the chair, 'we do the same thing. We have a funeral and we celebrate the human spirit—like with your mum, we'd talk about the things she did to make you happy, and the good times you had together, and the Merlin rug she made for you, and everything happy and fun we can remember.'

'Then we'd bury her?'

No fool, this kid, Tom thought, and felt a twinge of pride in his protégé.

'It's only her body we bury, because when you die your spirit leaves your body so all the fun parts and memories stay on with all the people who knew your mum, and with you especially. And we have a choice of how we want our bodies to be treated when we die—if we want them buried or cremated, which is burnt. They're only like the shells we used to live in, like houses for our spirits, so it's not as if it's the person who's being buried or cremated, but we have to decide what we think your mum would have preferred to have happen to her body.'

Okay, so she'd taken a while to get there, but she'd made it, and this time Tom felt pride in Lauren for handling it so well.

So far so well!

At least Bobby hadn't belted her one!

'Do we have to watch?'

Tom wasn't sure how to take that question, Bobby's tone giving no indication of his preference.

'Only if you want to,' Lauren told him. 'If you want to go to the funeral then that's fine, we'll all go, but you don't actually see the fire with a cremation.'

'That's good because she wouldn't like to be buried, I know,' Bobby declared, 'but I want to go and I want to sing her song.'

'What song is that?' asked Tom.

'It's about a rainbow and a fat man from that place where the surfers all go sings it, and it's Mum's favourite.'

Tom looked blankly at Lauren, who smiled— an ordinary, everyday Lauren smile that for some reason made his heart clench and his stomach knot and a kind of panic start inside him.

"'Somewhere over the Rainbow',' she was saying while his panic attack continued. 'A Hawaiian man sings it with "What a Wonderful World" like a medley. Joan used to bring the CD to the refuge. It could be in with her things.'

She gave Bobby a hug and promised him they'd sort it out, while Tom wondered if he could sort out what was happening to him.

Perhaps if he went to work…

Was it because he'd expected Lauren to feel a little awkward this morning but hadn't considered how he, himself, might feel that seeing an ordinary Lauren smile had sent him into a spin?

It couldn't be love.

He didn't do love.

Love was destructive.

Love had killed his parents and his sister, the sister he'd loved.

And evidence of love's destructive force was right here in front of him—in an orphaned child, although maybe Greg's feelings for Joan had been more about control than love.

But evidence of love was definitely there in

Bobby, the child talking of the song his mother had loved—a little boy wanting to show his love by singing it for her...

'I'm going to work!'

It was an abrupt departure—too abrupt—but he couldn't be worried about that. He had to get off the veranda before the tears pricking at his eyes at the image of the eight-year-old singing about rainbows—singing about hope———came streaming down his cheeks...

CHAPTER TEN

TOM must be regretting it, thought Lauren. How could he not be? A man like Tom, used to experienced, sophisticated women who could probably offer him all kinds of sensual pleasure, having to concentrate solely on her!

'School today!'

Lauren stopped staring after Tom's departing figure and concentrated on Bobby.

'You *want* to go to school?'

Bobby nodded, then added, 'But I have to take something to share to eat, like cake. It's last day so we play games and have a party and watermelon then we have watermelon fights.'

Lauren forgot her own problems and smiled, remembering the last day of summer term when she'd been at school. Definitely watermelon fights but there was no time to bake a cake.

'Come on, then,' she said to Bobby, 'Get ready

and we'll call at the bakery on the way and get a cake.'

Bobby sped away, appearing minutes later in his new jeans and tasselled shirt and cowboy hat and, no, she didn't have the heart to object for all she knew he'd get cake and watermelon over all of it.

'Can I tell them about the funeral?' he asked, as they drove down to the town.

Was this normal?

How did one know?

'Of course,' she told him, 'but as we haven't made all the arrangements, you can't tell people a date. Just say we'll put a notice in the paper.'

Silence, then one small hand crept onto her lap.

'You and Tom'll do that? You'll do the notice and…?'

She stopped the car for his voice had thickened, and she put her arms around him, assuring him they'd do the lot, he had no need to worry.

'And you'll take me?'

'Of course we will,' she said, hugging him to her and sniffing madly. 'We'll be right there beside you all the time.'

Choosing a cake soon took precedence over gloomy thoughts of funerals, so the little boy who marched proudly through the school gates in his new gear, Lauren by his side with the chocolate cake, had all of Bobby's old swagger, something his teacher noticed right away, greeting him warmly then sending him off to find his friends.

He raced away, then came bounding back.

'You know we get out early on last day,' he said to Lauren, and although they'd never got around to discussing her collecting him from school, she felt a thrill of pleasure that he'd assumed it would happen.

'What time?' Lauren asked his teacher, who was obviously dying to ask questions about Bobby's future but didn't want to intrude.

'Any time after one,' the teacher said, then she touched Lauren on the arm. 'He needs normality, that little boy.'

Lauren nodded, but as she walked back to the car, doubts descended.

She and Tom were hardly normality.

And this temporary situation wasn't normal.

Stability was normal—that's what Bobby needed.

Could she adopt him on her own?

Fired with determination to sort things out, she

drove directly to the hospital where she settled at her desk and phoned Mike.

'What's happening? Who's in charge of finding a relative for Bobby? Who do I need to speak to, to regularise his temporary care with me?'

Mike provided phone numbers but offered no joy as far as relatives were concerned. As far as anyone could discover, Bobby *had* no relatives.

The woman at Children's Services was harassed.

'You've no idea how many families break up over Christmas,' she muttered at Lauren. 'He's fine to stay with you for the moment but his name must be somewhere in the system so someone will eventually be in touch with you. There's all kinds of official stuff to go through to make him a ward of the state, which he'll have to be.'

'Over my dead body!' Lauren said, slamming down the phone and startling the occupational therapist who was walking past the door, and making Tom, who'd come through the door, raise an eyebrow.

'Over your dead body?'

'Some stupid woman talking about making Bobby a ward of the state,' Lauren told him, so angry she was surprised she couldn't see wisps of steam rising in the air around her head.

Tom came further into the room and pulled up a chair to sit across the desk from her.

'He probably will have to be made a ward of the state before we can officially adopt him, and if you think about it, you'll know that's right,' he said, as calmly as if they were carrying on some conversation they'd begun earlier, 'but it doesn't have to happen right now and, anyway, it's only paperwork.'

'What did you say?'

Lauren spaced out the words so he'd have no trouble hearing them.

The eyebrow lifted.

'About him being made a ward of the state? It's only paperwork?' Tom asked.

More wisps of steam!

'You know I don't mean that!' she growled. 'I mean the bit about our adopting him. *Our* adopting him!'

He grinned at her and although her anger was still simmering nicely, the grin did distract her, sending tremors of a desire she'd never felt before—strong physical desire—through her body.

'I thought about it as I walked over to the hospital earlier. Bobby's happy with us, and he's a kid who deserves a break. I think between the two of us, we could do a good job with him. We'd probably have to get married to make the officials feel more comfortable, but I can't see that being too big a problem—'

He broke off so the grin could come back—widening into a teasing smile that sent molten spears of longing sizzling down her nerves.

She had to forget last night and spears of longing and concentrate on practical matters—except she couldn't find what practical matter she wanted to concentrate on.

Marriage?

'You don't want to get married!' she reminded him. 'You've held forth often enough on your single-and-loving-it philosophy. You've never pushed your ideas on other people, but you've made it very plain that marriage and children weren't in your long-term plan for a happy life, while as for love—a destructive force, I think you called it.'

He was silent for so long she wondered if she should have kept her mouth shut, but the marrying idea had come so out of the blue she could barely think, let alone express her disbelief more rationally.

And there was another problem with the whole situation—the problem of a little bit of her skittering around in an excited tizzy and bouncing up and down in delight, twittering 'marriage' into her befuddled brain.

'I did love someone once,' Tom finally said, jolting Lauren back to earth, the excited twitter firmly squelched. 'My sister Jane. And she loved me! It didn't matter how our parents fought, Jane was there to shield me, and to hug me and tell me things would be all right.'

He paused, and Lauren waited.

'Bobby hasn't got a Jane, but he has got us. I know we can't wipe away what he's suffered emotionally and possibly physically over the years, but by giving him the best possible life we can offer, surely we can help him forget a lot of it.'

So the excited bit had got it wrong, Lauren realised, but she also realised that if she hadn't known she loved this man before this moment, she knew she loved him now. Sitting there, offering his future to a little boy, committing himself to love the child, how could she not love Tom?

But wouldn't loving him make what he was asking harder?

Loving him, could she marry him, knowing he didn't love her?

He'd loved his sister once, and Lauren was reasonably sure he was growing fonder and fonder of Bobby—heading towards love—but he didn't love her.

And why should he?

But marriage without love?

For the sake of a child?

How confused could one woman get?

'A relative might turn up,' she said, desperate to shift the conversation to somewhere she might be able to get a grasp on it.

Tom frowned at her.

'You don't *want* to keep him?'

Lauren thought of the way the little boy's hand would creep into hers, and the warmth she felt in her body when he did that.

'Of course I want to keep him,' she muttered at Tom. 'It's all this marriage stuff that's got me stymied.'

Then a thought occurred to her, and although she

knew she'd flush scarlet as she asked, she knew she had to raise the subject.

'This isn't some noble gesture on your part after our—we—after we—after last night?' she finally managed, and he laughed.

'Darling Lauren, if I proposed to every woman I'd slept with I'd have been incarcerated for polygamy long ago.' He paused then his face grew serious. 'Though speaking of last night, you're okay?'

He reached across the desk and took her hand, which she'd stupidly left lying on some papers in the middle of it.

'No regrets?' he pressed, squeezing her fingers and looking into her eyes as heat swept through her.

She shook her head and tried to mumble something about last night not being anything to do with anything, but he laughed again.

'You don't think so?' he teased. 'Don't you think it's quite important that a married couple enjoy each other in bed?'

He'd turned her hand and was tickling her palm with his thumb and she could barely sit still in her chair, so erotic was this simple touch, but the 'married' thing was still haunting her. There had to be another way. Tom didn't really want to be tied down in marriage and she wasn't going to—couldn't, she rather thought—marry someone who didn't love her...

Could she?

'I'd better get back to work before we do something we shouldn't do right here on your desk,' he said, giving her fingers a final squeeze and walking briskly from the room, stopping in the door to add, 'See you tonight,' in a voice that sent further shivers down her spine.

Lauren, deciding it was impossible to even attempt to sort out her feelings about whatever was going on between her and Tom, went off to visit Alyssa, who was feeling much more comfortable and talking about taking Karen back to the US with her and the children.

'My dad's coming over, you see,' she explained to Lauren. 'I'd lost touch with him—well, it was hard because he hated Nat right from the start—but now we can begin again, Dad and me, and Karen's never travelled and if she's not at home, Nat can't take out his anger on her. She was telling me she wants to give her place to the refuge and the woman who's always worked for her will stay on so someone knows the feeding routine and how the farm-stay business runs.'

Lauren smiled.

'I see you've got it all worked out,' she said.

'Thanks to you,' Alyssa told her. 'You've no idea what having clean hair and some moisturiser did for my confidence. I'm sad about the baby but maybe that's for the best, too. I've known for ages I should leave Nat but I didn't dare. Known I should report him, too, but he kept promising... Anyway, now, with Dad and Karen by my side, I know I can do both and I can make a new life for me and the girls.'

Lauren bent and kissed Alyssa's cheek.

'I'm sure you can,' she whispered. 'You deserve happiness in life, everyone does, so go after it.'

Go after it?

The words echoed in her head as she drove to collect Bobby from school.

But would marrying Tom be going after happiness, or going after pain?

Didn't love need to be returned?

Bobby was waiting at the school gate, a cardboard box at his feet.

'I got this from my teacher. She was going to throw them out and I know where Mum kept the decorations at home so can we go and get them 'cos Tom's got none at his place and next week's Christmas.'

Bobby's rush of words left Lauren nearly as confused as Tom's marriage conversation had earlier, only less inwardly distracted.

'Decorations, for Christmas,' Bobby repeated, and Lauren caught on.

'We'll have to see Mike at the police station. He's got your mother's house keys,' she said.

'I know where the spare one is,' Bobby offered. 'Mum left one out for me in case she mightn't be at home.'

So! No reprieve of driving to the station and talking to Mike.

Lauren studied the excited child.

'You're sure about this?' she asked, taking a rather grubby hand in both of hers. 'Sure you'll be okay going into the house with your mum not there?'

Bobby looked at her, his blue eyes filling with tears.

'I gotta do stuff like that!' he muttered angrily. 'Like the funeral too!'

'Oh, Bobby!' Lauren whispered, and she pulled him into her arms and cried with him.

But as it turned out they didn't have to do 'stuff like that' for two of the women who knew Joan from the refuge were at the house, and all Joan's belongings were already packed.

'The landlord wanted the place emptied,' one of the women explained to Lauren, 'so we thought we'd pack it all up and keep it for whenever Bobby might want it. These boxes here are his toys and books.'

'And decorations?' Bobby demanded, and one of the women produced another box, probably labelled by Joan herself.

They helped Lauren load Bobby's boxes and the decorations into the car, promising to find room to store the rest, and Lauren drove home, insisting Bobby keep his seat belt on as he rummaged through the boxes in search of forgotten treasures.

The house was empty and although Lauren had grave doubts about decorating Tom's house without his permission, nothing was going to stop Bobby.

First he opened the box he'd brought from school, digging through the contents.

'We had a real tree at school. A tree in a pot, but Mrs Stoddart must'a taken it home. We need a tree.'

'Can't we just put up decorations?' Lauren asked.

Bobby sent her a pitying look.

'Where will Santa put the presents if there isn't a tree?' he demanded, and a new worry surfaced in Lauren's head.

Presents!

They'd have to get presents for Bobby.

More than a stocking filled with oddments, for sure!

What's more, they'd have to figure out what he might have asked Santa to give him.

Lauren's mind was jerking around like a chicken in search of seed, until Bobby's voice brought her to the present.

''Cos we don't have chimneys for Santa to come down here at the Cove, we have to have trees,' the boy causing most of her confusion—though not all—informed her.

'Right, a tree,' Lauren said. 'Does it have to be

live or can we go and get one of those green ones from one of the shops in the mall?'

Bobby considered this for a while.

'I s'pose one of them would do, but it should be real,' he told her.

What had he said earlier?

Mrs Stoddart had a tree in a pot.

'Okay,' Lauren told him. 'Let's go to the nursery and see what we can find. Once we get the tree we'll know how many decorations we need for it.'

'Could we get some lights for outside while we're out?'

Images of tremendously decorated houses— houses that won prizes for their Christmas light displays—flashed through Lauren's mind.

'Maybe just a few lights,' she agreed.

Perhaps because he was used to not getting everything he wanted, Bobby didn't argue and they set off to buy a tree, Bobby choosing a four-foot-high Norfolk pine, then to the mall where, to Bobby's credit, it was Lauren who went mad.

Why *not* get two small light-outlined reindeer to put out the front? And as for the blow-up Santa, well, he could sit on the veranda, while the strings of lights with smaller strings dripping off them would look fantastic stretched along the eaves.

They staggered home to find Tom staring at the contents of the boxes they'd half-unpacked.

'Christmas decorations?' he said, his voice so carefully neutral Lauren had a moment's panic.

'You don't like them?'

Had he heard that panic in her voice that he smiled and touched her gently on the arm?

'How would I know whether I like them or not when I've never had them in my own home?'

Lauren blew out the breath she'd been holding and smiled back at him.

'That's good because there's a few more bits and pieces in the car.'

Four hours later, having stopped only briefly to consume the casserole that had finally been cooked, they finished the decorating.

'Turn the lights on, turn them on!'

Bobby was bouncing up and down with excitement, but Tom refused to press the switch connected to the various power-boards spread around the house.

'I think you should do it,' he said, and the blatant

adoration in the little boy's face as he looked at Tom caught at Lauren's heart.

He pressed the switch and the lights came on slowly. The strings of blue and red and green changing colour all the time so they looked like water dancing in a coloured fountain. The two little reindeer nodded at each other on the front lawn, one dropping his head lower, perhaps pretending to eat moss. Santa, to everyone's surprise, not only lit up from inside, but began to 'Ho, ho, ho' in fine spirit and the star Tom had somehow affixed above the front entrance flashed its brightness to the town below.

'It's beautiful!'

Awe filled Bobby's voice, and Lauren, slipping her arm around his shoulder, had to agree.

'Tomorrow we'll do inside,' Bobby announced, and now Lauren glanced at Tom.

'Okay with you?' she asked.

He nodded.

'As long as there aren't too many lights,' he told them. 'This is an old house and the power supply's already under strain.'

'Just on the tree—one string. Mum's had them

for ages,' Bobby declared, and Tom agreed one more string of lights wouldn't hurt.

He'd moved, so he, too, had his arm around Bobby, his hand touching Lauren's arm, the three of them linked.

A family?

That's what Bobby needed.

And continuity. His mother's string of Christmas lights on the tree each year, the new decorations going up. It was about continuity and knowing now what she did about Tom she could understand why he'd felt their marriage would be the answer for Bobby. The little boy would have a real family—one for life—not a series of so-called 'families'—being moved on for whatever reason.

But marriage?

She could see Tom's point of view that only with their marriage could Bobby have the security he needed, so why was she hesitating?

Surely not because she, who'd never considered marriage as an option in her future, was suddenly quibbling over a marriage without love?

They turned out the lights and went inside, falling easily into Bobby's bedtime routine, Lauren's turn to read the story.

Tom was gone when she came out of Bobby's bedroom, presumably called back to the hospital, and instead of worrying over love and marriage she turned her attention to practical matters, putting Bobby's dirty clothes into the laundry, emptying his school-bag of books and notes and clutter, wondering how on earth they could find out what he wanted for Christmas, wondering if he'd object if she suggested he take a turn on Santa's knee at the local mall—surely Santa had some way of passing on requests.

She was smoothing out the papers from his school-bag, checking each before she tossed them, in case there might be something important there.

And there was!

An envelope addressed in an adult hand to Tom and Lauren, and inside another envelope with 'Santa' scrawled across it in red felt pen.

Lauren slit the second envelope open, unfolding the piece of paper inside.

'Dear Santa,
For Christmas I would like a bike with red weels and red handl bars and red pedls and

a nice dress for Mum and for her and Greg
to stop yelling.

Yor frend

Bobby'

Lauren smoothed her fingers over the paper
again and again, barely aware of the mess her
splotches of tears were making on the words. She
was still sitting there, still weeping, when Tom
came in.

'I'll marry you,' she said, sniffing loudly then
dashing her wrist across her eyes in the hope of
stopping the tears.

'Well, I'm glad I've made you so happy,' Tom
teased, but his grey eyes were full of concern as
he came towards her, squatting by her side and
taking her restless hands in his.

'We must promise never to yell,' Lauren added,
looking at the face of the man she loved. 'No
matter what, no yelling.'

'I can handle that,' Tom said gently, then he
leaned forward and kissed her on the lips.

'And we've got to find a red bike for him,' she
added, and Tom, deciding that the only way he'd
make sense of what was going on was to read what-

ever had upset Lauren in the first place, removed the piece of paper she held in trembling fingers and read the letter. Then he stood up, hauled Lauren from the chair, and hugged her tightly.

'You're a good woman, Lauren Cooper,' he whispered in her ear. 'A special woman.'

He'd have liked to add how special he found her, to have talked of love, but his realisation of love—his about-face acceptance of it as anything other than a destructive force—was too new, too fragile, to be brought out into the open. Besides which, talk of love might totally freak Lauren out, just when she seemed to be agreeing to his marriage idea.

So he held her, hoping he might be able to tell her without words, wondering if his adoration of her body, something he intended showing her very soon, would make her realise how he felt.

'We need to find a red bike. I can hardly take Bobby shopping with me to look for one. What should we do?'

Tom eased away and put his hand beneath her chin to tilt her face up towards his.

'You're thinking bikes and I'm thinking love!'

Whoops!

He had no idea how the word had slipped out, but now it hung, like the fat blow-up Santa, in the air between them.

'Love?' Lauren echoed, so uncertainly Tom *had* to hug her again.

'Yes, love,' he whispered. 'A four-letter word I'd never thought I'd find a use for, but having found you and Bobby there's no other word to cover it.'

He eased away again and once more tilted up her face to he could look into those clear hazel eyes.

'Do you mind very much?' he asked, and saw her frown.

'Mind what?'

Nerves churned in his stomach. In fact, he was reasonably certain that if he raced off and threw up he'd feel a darned sight better, but now he'd started with this love thing he'd better keep at it.

'Mind my loving you?'

Could she hear the uncertainty in his voice—the fear?

She looked more puzzled than she had earlier, clear eyes clouding over as she kind of squinted at him.

'You love me?' she queried, definitely disbelieving.

Tom straightened up—it was time to show some spine.

'I do,' he said firmly, and just to prove it, he kissed her.

Hard!

Then hot!

Then heavy as his body took control and claimed her mouth, consuming it as if he could take her into his skin and be one with her.

Her response didn't exactly say she loved him, but it certainly indicated she didn't mind his kisses. Right now there was the question of love...

One-sided love?

Surely she could have said 'I love you', or even 'Me too' when he'd said he loved her, but no, when she did speak it was to ask if he knew of any bicycle shops in Port that might stay open late at Christmas time, adding, 'Because we could get Cam and Jo to babysit and drive down to get the bike, but we should phone first to make sure they've got a red one of the kind an eight-year-old would want.'

'You want to drive to Port to buy a bike?'

He'd eased away from her, needing distance so his brain would work.

'Not necessarily tonight,' she said in a kindly voice. 'But we need to know what evenings they'll be open and we need to find out if we can get one already put together. My brother bought one for his son and it took until dawn on Christmas morning to put it together and even then it went backwards because he'd done something wrong with the chain.'

Tom slumped into a chair.

'Did you miss the bit of conversation earlier when I said I loved you?' he demanded.

Her face went still, then she shook her head.

'No, I heard it,' she said, 'but I thought it might be best not to talk about it in case it was an aberration.'

For a man who'd never done the love declaration before, the conversation was becoming unnecessarily convoluted.

'Me loving you an aberration or me saying it an aberration?'

Lauren shrugged.

'Either, I suppose, or maybe both. I just thought if I didn't mention it then it could just go away, and anyway the bike *is* important, you know. It's in Bobby's letter to Santa.'

She passed him a scrappy piece of paper she must have had crumpled in one hand all this time and he smoothed it out and read it, swallowing hard when he'd finished.

'We won't yell,' he promised Lauren, who nodded back at him.

'And we'll find a bike.'

She nodded again, and Tom knew it was now or never.

'So,' he said, 'with that sorted, let's get back to love.'

Did she cringe?

Was she afraid to tell him she didn't love him?

The thought brought a wave of panic through his body and all but melted his brain, but he stiffened, told himself to be a man, and waited.

And waited...

'You want me to start?' he finally asked, although he felt that was wrong because he'd already said it, but what the hell, here it went.

'I love you, Lauren,' he said, loud and clear, adding a kind of addendum to the original idea by saying, 'I think maybe I have for a while—kind of loved you anyway, but wary of seeing more of you, seeing you romantically, in case it *was* love, and I was so convinced I couldn't do love I steered clear.'

She smiled and stepped a little closer. Close enough to touch but not touching.

'Do you know when you get excited about something you trip over your words?' she teased, using words he'd said to her some days ago. 'But I love you too. And like you, I think it was probably there for a while, but feeling how I did about intimacy, I didn't want to let you down.'

'As if you could ever let me down,' Tom told her, gathering her into his arms and holding her carefully, as if she was a precious object that might shatter with too much pressure. 'As if you could ever let anyone down! You're kind and good and thoughtful and loving and probably far too good for me, but you and me, we're all Bobby's got so maybe we're stuck with each other.'

And with that he kissed her, gently at first, letting the embers of their physical love flare gradually back to life, igniting them both so they were sliding fingers onto skin beneath frustrating clothes when a 'Bleagh!' from the doorway had them springing apart.

Tom recovered first, holding out his arm to bring Bobby into the circle of their love.

'Get used to the sloppy stuff, kid,' he said, 'there's going to be a lot of it around.'

And Lauren proved it, by hugging Bobby hard and kissing his unruly hair and then his ear and then his cheek until he squirmed and shrieked in protest and Tom knew he'd found a family...

CHAPTER ELEVEN

LOOKING back, Lauren realised that the big mistake they made was leaving Bobby with Jo and Cam while they drove to Port to buy a red bike. Two nights before Christmas and the shops were open until midnight. Not only that, but all the Christmas decorations were reduced in price and she discovered for the first time how much the man she loved loved a bargain.

'What on earth...?' Jo demanded, as they began staggering into the house laden with boxes and bags of decorations.

'He likes a sale,' Lauren explained, looking helplessly at the pile of new acquisitions. 'We're never going to get them all up.'

Tom came in, Cam following with the last of the purchases.

'I've put the bike over in my office at the hospital,' he told Lauren, then he looked at the two women. 'Well, what are you waiting for? Do you think these decorations are going to hang themselves?'

'You want to do them tonight? It's nearly midnight,' Lauren protested.

Tom shot her a quick grin.

'This from a woman who had me knotting a rug at two in the morning!'

'Knotting a rug?' Jo echoed feebly, looking from one to the other then shaking her head, while Cam was already digging decorations out of boxes, demanding scissors and insisting they all get busy.

'Think how Bobby will love it when he wakes up,' Tom whispered to Lauren, standing so close she could feel the tendrils of warmth and love wrapping around them once again.

'Fair enough,' she said, and she joined the others, until the whole house was hung with decorations, a giant paper bell over the dining table, mistletoe over every doorway—Jo and Cam taking far too much advantage of that—the tree alight, in spite of Tom's misgivings, with bright balls of glistening colour. Every window had its own frame of tinsel, the veranda railings were wound with greenery, and up on the roof—though what two respected medicos were doing on a roof in the middle of the night!—was a full team of reindeer and a sleigh big enough to hold the blow-up Santa Lauren and Bobby had bought earlier.

Once it was done, they sat down to enjoy a cold drink, the pleasure they would give the little boy warming all of them.

'So much has happened,' Jo mused, 'since the stands went down. What could have been a terrible accident minimised by Tom and Cam's fast action.'

'We were lucky,' Tom said. 'All but one of the patients have been discharged and he'll be home for Christmas.'

'Bobby wasn't so lucky,' Lauren reminded them.

'Not in losing his mother,' Jo said, 'that was terrible, but then look where he ended up—with two of the most loving people in the whole Cove. Yes, he'll grieve and you'll both help him keep his mother's memory alive, but for the rest of his life you'll be the only parents he knows.'

'Which is a very scary thought,' Tom said, but he reached out and took Lauren's hand, adding, with a smile, 'Although it's kind of exciting, too, isn't it?'

She leant across and kissed him on the lips.

'Very exciting,' she said.

'Well, there's a nice surprise,' Jo said, standing up and tugging Cam to his feet. 'Methinks it's time we left these two to talk about parenthood.'

'Should we?' Tom asked when they'd departed.

'Should we what? Talk about parenthood? Or maybe go to bed?' Lauren teased.

'Minx!' Tom said, taking her in his arms, his heart—his entire body—so full of pleasure or gratitude or maybe love that she could tease him like that it was a wonder he could speak at all.

She nestled closer.

'We've the rest of our lives to talk about parenthood,' she whispered.

'And to go to bed,' he answered, adding even more quietly, 'Together!'

Bobby's delight the next morning made all the work they'd done the night before worthwhile, and that evening, Christmas Eve, as they stood by the tree on the foreshore, singing carols, they could look up and see their Santa in his sleigh, and the star shining right on the apex of the roof, guiding them home.

The damaged stands had been cleared away earlier in the week, but they stood on the other side of the tree, Bobby between them, his high, sweet voice rising to the heavens, his electric candle held steady in his hands.

Tom looked down at him, then at Lauren, with her arm around the child's shoulders, then he turned to look out at the ocean and knew he'd come home. After all his wanderings, he'd finally come home, and not only had he found a home, he'd found a family to live in it, his family—his loves!

Had Lauren caught his thoughts that she turned towards him and the hand that had been resting on Bobby's shoulder reached out to touch grasp his fingers?

'I love you.'

She mouthed the words above Bobby's head and squeezed his fingers.

'And me you,' he said, but he spoke aloud, making Bobby turn towards him.

'What?' the child demanded, and Tom knelt in front of him.

'I was just saying "I love you",' he told the little

boy, then before Bobby could protest he kissed hr quickly on the cheek.

The carols ended, and with arms wrapped around each other they walked home up the hill. Home to the Christmas lights and the star of hope—home to the future.

Together!

* * * * *

Mills & Boon® *Large Print Medical*

July

THE BOSS SHE CAN'T RESIST	Lucy Clark
HEART SURGEON, HERO...HUSBAND?	Susan Carlisle
DR LANGLEY: PROTECTOR OR PLAYBOY?	Joanna Neil
DAREDEVIL AND DR KATE	Leah Martyn
SPRING PROPOSAL IN SWALLOWBROOK	Abigail Gordon
DOCTOR'S GUIDE TO DATING IN THE JUNGLE	Tina Beckett

August

SYDNEY HARBOUR HOSPITAL: LILY'S SCANDAL	Marion Lennox
SYDNEY HARBOUR HOSPITAL: ZOE'S BABY	Alison Roberts
GINA'S LITTLE SECRET	Jennifer Taylor
TAMING THE LONE DOC'S HEART	Lucy Clark
THE RUNAWAY NURSE	Dianne Drake
THE BABY WHO SAVED DR CYNICAL	Connie Cox

September

FALLING FOR THE SHEIKH SHE SHOULDN'T	Fiona McArthur
DR CINDERELLA'S MIDNIGHT FLING	Kate Hardy
BROUGHT TOGETHER BY BABY	Margaret McDonagh
ONE MONTH TO BECOME A MUM	Louisa George
SYDNEY HARBOUR HOSPITAL: LUCA'S BAD GIRL	Amy Andrews
THE FIREBRAND WHO UNLOCKED HIS HEART	Anne Fraser

'Turn the lights on, turn them on!'

Bobby was bouncing up and down with excitement, but Tom refused to press the switch connected to the various powerboards spread around the house.

'I think you should do it,' he said, and the blatant adoration in the little boy's face as he looked at Tom caught at Lauren's heart.

He pressed the switch and the lights came slowly on. The strings of blue and red and green changed colour all the time, so they looked like water dancing in a coloured fountain. The two little reindeer nodded at each other on the front lawn, one dropping his head lower, perhaps pretending to eat moss. Santa, to everyone's surprise, not only lit up from inside, but began to 'Ho, Ho, Ho' in fine spirit, and the star Tom had somehow affixed above the front entrance flashed its brightness to the town below.

'It's beautiful!'

Awe filled Bobby's voice, and Lauren, slipping her arm around his shoulder, had to agree.

Tom had moved, so he, too, had his arm around Bobby, his hand touching Lauren's arm, the three of them linked.

A family?

That was what Bobby needed.